FRAMED

Framed

CREAGH MANNING

Wattle Arts

For Julie.

Chapter One

Clay threw back his head and inhaled Melbourne's cool night air. The inrush of air conflated his mild champagne euphoria into drunkenness and his head spun as he stepped into Church Street from Waltham Place. Unsteady on his feet, he turned 360 degrees to get his bearings. That went well, Clay thought as he set off down Church Street towards Swan Street.

Everything sold. All his paintings in Julia's Autumn Charity Exhibition were snapped up by eager buyers. It had surprised him and lifted his mood. Soon he'd have to stop referring to himself as a little-known emerging artist.

He'd resisted Julia's formal offer of a lift to his studio in Richmond. Julia regarded the industrial district south of Swan Street, where his studio was, as too dangerous to wander at night. For a lone female, yeah, he agreed. It was true that some of Melbourne's most notorious crime families lived there. But Clay had never encountered any of those nefarious characters. Either they were rare or chose not to shit in their own nest.

However, the real reason he chose to walk was to avoid encouraging too much alone time with Julia. He'd been there and done that, and now that she managed the sale of his art, he preferred a simple business relationship. So, he'd told her a small white lie, said he needed the exercise.

It was two thirty in the morning and his walk along Church Street's deserted footpaths, between hibernating buildings, and beside empty tramlines, presented a cityscape of grisaille stillness, which reminded him of how a good painting could capture a frozen moment.

Elated by the vision and increasingly tipsy, Clay revelled in the walk down Church Street. In a moment of bravado, he leapt onto the low blue stone garden wall fronting St. Stephen's, to tightrope walk along its apex. Balance gained from years of surfing helped him progress fearlessly until he tried a pirouette manoeuvre. As he spun, his right, white Zodiac loafer flew off, disappearing into the bushes of St. Stephen's front garden. Clumsy searching proved futile, but the loss of his shoe failed to dampen his mood. He continued to fence-top-walk one shoe short.

A few dollops of rain spattered Clay's forehead as he arrived at Swan Street. He was halfway home. Only an odd wisp of dark cloud drifted overhead dispelling any concern about getting drenched. No cloud was opaque enough to obscure the large Swiss cheddar moon glimpsed between buildings as he walked. As if drawn by this moon, Clay quickened his pace down Swan Street towards Richmond Station.

When he emerged from beneath the Swan Street rail bridge, he propped mid-stride, transfixed by the view of the Melbourne skyline. The full moon hung in the north east, adding a side light to the gentle glow emanating from the city's massed skyscrapers. A transcendent moment, a sublime vision to cap off a great night. He could never have imagined that he would end up with a successful, enjoyable career, purely by chance. Life was good.

The onset of heavier rain, dampened Clay's reverie and prompted him to get a move on. He pulled his shirt up over his head, turned into Cremorne Street, and commenced a stumbling jog towards Cubitt Street. By the time he arrived at his studio, those few scudding clouds he'd seen earlier, were dumping torrents on him. Clay giggled like a schoolboy as he skipped through the puddles down Cubitt Street towards Cotton Lane. Along the way, he lost his shirt to the wind but laughed it off. Now soaked to the skin, he didn't give a toss. Life was better than good.

Clay's fingertips caressed the embossed brass plaque above his studio door mail slot.

Clay Weston — Artist.

He smiled as he admired the surface of the steel-faced door. Light from an adjacent Cotton Lane street-lamp revealed the door's texture and exaggerated the muscles across his rain-soaked back the way a raking light revealed an underpainting's hidden brushwork. His attention soon returned to reality, when he discovered, that he'd not only lost his shoe and shirt on the jaunt home. Somehow, he'd also lost his leather shoulder satchel, which contained his wallet and keys. Must have left it back at the gallery, he thought.

Now Clay stared at the keyed deadlock below his name plaque and wondered with half-drunken detachment whether he could pick the lock. Nope, not a chance; he wouldn't have a clue how to start. At the same time, Clay's artist's right brain, bored with the problem of gaining entry, became fascinated with the sinewy curve of the door handle. He stroked it lovingly.

An avalanche of cold water from the flooded roof gutter above dispelled his aesthetic reverie. The stream of water plastered Clay's normally surf-bleached curls flat against his forehead. Clay felt like a drowned biscuit, and he thought, if the rain didn't stop soon, he'd start to resemble one of Dali's melted clocks.

Steel bars over the wire-reinforced frosted glass windows on either side of the door dispelled any hope of front access. Clay rummaged through his sodden memory for an alternative. Eventually, he remembered the studio's rarely used loading bay doors in the old dunnyman's lane, known as Little Cotton Way. Clay shuffled around the corner of the building into Little Cotton Way, where he was surprised to see his life model's familiar pink Fiat Bambino parked in front of the doors. His surprise was soon replaced with frustration when he remembered that the blocked loading bay doors were padlocked on the inside. Clay stomped back into Cotton Lane, his earlier good mood a distant memory. Clay lost it with the door.

'Fucking hell! A couple of lousy drinks and I'm stuck out here wallowing in the gutter.'

Clay stared at the door in frustration. But the blank response from the door seemed to match that of his brain. God knows; he'd been wasted often enough in the past when depressed, but not for ages, not since his recent successes. He'd have deserved this frustration if he'd truly fallen off the wagon.

Clay flicked his head back to clear strands of wet hair from his eyes, but also to clear the leaden self-pity engulfing his thoughts. The door unmoved, stared back at him like a blank canvas. Clay tried to think. If he'd left his satchel containing his wallet and keys at the gallery, could he return and retrieve them? No, probably not, because the gallery would be closed, and Julia would have gone home. What other options did he have? Clay allowed his mind to empty, hoping for a creative cog to drop. He stared hard at the door. Slowly, the door's scratched and rust-stained surface conjured up an image of a naked girl. A pleasant but ridiculous distraction until it dawned on him that he knew and recognised the girl. Clay knew the tanned tones of her skin, the singular proportion of her limbs and the distinctive shape of her face with its symmetrical features. Knowledge, he'd gleaned from many hours spent observing his model, Pamela.

Clay had painted her yesterday, and he remembered offering her a place to crash for the night as he'd rushed out to attend the charity exhibition and after-party at Blakely Gallery. Pam's little car was still there, parked around the corner. Maybe. Just maybe, she was still inside, asleep in the loft at the back of his studio.

Pam could let him in.

With renewed purpose, Clay pounded on the door, yelling her name through the mail slot, and then pausing to listen.

'Pam. Pamela love, are you there?'

With no answer from behind the door, Clay's frustration increased. It seemed to Clay that the rain, rattling noisily on the iron roofs and pavements of Cotton Lane, increased in tempo every time he attacked the door.

'Christ! She'll never hear me,' Clay cursed, kicking at the door.

Bad idea.

Clay's toes on his socked right foot flamed with pain. He hopped from foot to foot doing a demented war dance to his lost shoe. With his throbbing toes immersed in a stream of cold water flooding down Cotton Lane's bluestone gutter, the pain diminished, but not his frustration. Clay spotted a dislodged cobblestone in the gutter. Grabbing it he returned to the door with a crazed vigour and hammered away on the metal. Clay pounded and stopped to listen, and then pounded again before bending to press his ear into the mail slot, he heard only the sound of a blank canvas.

Pam had to be there. Clay believed she would never have left without her car. She had to be asleep in the loft at the rear of his studio. To wake her, Clay had to project the sound of his presence towards the loft. Clay was winding up to hurl the cobblestone towards the rear of the tin roof when he noticed a change in the colour of the door. The water streaming down its surface took on an oscillating blue tinge. Clay moved in closer to examine the blue rivulets.

'Well, well, well. What have we here Officer Parker? A case of drunk and disorderly or an attempted break and enter?' Clay swung around to confront two police officers.

Detective Bill Walsh, a squat tank of a man in a damp-crumpled raincoat, protecting a balding head from the rain with a folded copy of The Sun, stood behind him on the footpath in front of a police car with a roof-mounted, rotating blue light. His partner, Senior Constable Jenny Parker, having just emerged from the driver's seat, struggled to make her weather poncho watertight, while trying to keep a powerful hand torch trained on Clay's face.

'It's my place. It's where I live,' Clay said, trying to unobtrusively lower the cobblestone. Clay raised his other arm to shield his eyes from the torchlight.

'Doesn't look much like a house,' Walsh said, pointing at the door. 'More like an office or a factory.'

'It's my studio.'

'Really! What sort of studio would that be around here? Massage studio?'

Parker stepped to the front of the police car and ran the torch beam down over Clay's soaked jeans to his socked foot then back up to settle on his broad chest.

'It's my painting studio.'

Walsh smirked and stepped into Clay's personal space.

'So, what's with the rock?' Walsh sniffed. 'Had a bit to drink, have we?'

'I may have. The party, I guess,' Clay said, stuttering for an explanation. 'I walked home, and now I find I don't have my wallet or keys.'

'So, no ID either?'

'No.'

'All right, let's have your name son?'

'Weston, Clay.'

'Not much help pal, I can see THAT on the door. So, where are we then?'

'Sixteen Cotton Lane, off Cubitt Street, Richmond.' Walsh peered left and right, then stalked down the lane to peer into Little Cotton Way. He spotted Pam's pink Bambino and turned back towards Clay.

'Your car, Mr. Weston?'

'Afraid not.'

'No rego we can check then?'

'Sorry.' Clay was beginning to feel like a Philistine in an art gallery.

'How about a driver's licence?'

'Ah yes, I do, but it's in my wallet, which I don't have.' Clay shrugged and stuffed his hands into his pockets. 'Anyway, it's been suspended.'

Walsh turned to his partner. 'If you can tear your torch beam away from his chest, I'll watch him while you check his details over the radio.'

Senior Constable Parker frowned at Detective Walsh, snapped off her torch and moved back to the police car.

The rain evaporated into a light drizzle impelled by an early morning southerly breeze. Clay wished he was catching waves at St. Kilda on the Bay. He began to shiver.

'If Parker finds you don't have a police record, then we'll help you with the door. Get you inside and out of the rain so you don't catch your death, eh?' Detective Walsh grinned, 'Can't do you for break and enter on your own place, can we?'

A set of lock pics from the glove box of the police car so easily opened Clay's front door for the detective, that he wondered why he'd rejected not trying to pick it himself earlier, or why he'd even bothered to lock the door in the first place.

Clay pushed past Detective Walsh and reached in to flick on the single naked light globe dangling from the ceiling. They entered what had once been the reception room of a light engineering business. Both Walsh and Parker scrutinised the entry as if expecting to find stolen goods. Instead, to the right they saw an empty dust-covered reception counter and leaning against the opposite wall; they saw a dusty stack of nondescript paintings in vintage frames. Detective Walsh peered and poked at the paintings as if he'd stumbled on an art heist.

'From deceased estates,' Clay said, standing in a drip puddle with the guilty need to offer an explanation. 'I buy paintings from the estates of unknown artists.'

'And?' Walsh asked, sensing Clay's unease.

'I reuse the canvases. You know, paint over the other artist's work...'

'Right...'

Clay winced, but the detective's expression betrayed no opinion on the merits of destroying another artist's entire life's work.

The detective's attention shifted.

'You live here?'

'Through there, out back.' Clay gathered up his mail, stepped across the entry and opened a door opposite, which led into what had once been the engineering workshop.

At 3AM on a cloudy and wet autumn night, little of Melbourne's city glow made it through the pigeon-soiled skylights. Clay snapped on a bank of fluros. The rectangular factory space flickered into soft relief. The building's red double-brick walls displayed exposed plumbing, wiring and exhaust ducting. Almost four metres above the heavily planked and oil-stained wooden floor, cobwebbed timber trusses supported grey galvanised corrugated iron. Clay's sleeping loft occupied the rear end of the space. Clay had installed a plaster ceiling over the loft area, which was divided into two rooms by movable partitions. A salvaged red steel fire escape ladder provided access.

The place was comfortable; certainly not a chic industrial conversion, it had been a utilitarian renovation. Beneath the loft were timber storage racks loaded with Clay's paintings.

To the left of the entrance stood two large studio easels, surrounded by workbenches covered with paint tubes, pots of brushes, rags, cans of thinners, a large paint-encrusted palette, and drawings on large sheets of Arches cartridge paper.

Cold and wet, Clay drip-toed across the paint spattered-floor, dropped his mail on the end of a bench and grabbed a clean but paint-stained smock. Wrapped in the smock he turned with renewed confidence to engage the two police officers, who'd propped just inside the entrance.

They stood staring.

'What's that smell?' Senior Constable Parker said holding a finger under her nose.

'Gum turpentine and linseed', Clay said, looking toward the loft and wondering if Pamela was up there.

Detective Walsh stepped up to the nearest easel and pulled off the dust cover to reveal an almost life-sized nude painting of Pamela.

'We could do him for pornography,' he said, testing the surface of the painting with his finger as if about to taste cake icing.

'I dunno,' Senior Constable Parker said, 'depends on what she's doing with that duck.'

'It's a swan. You know, Leda and the swan, from Greek mythology,' Clay said.

'Oh! It's swan porn, not duck porn!' Walsh said, winking at Parker.

'I guess, given half a chance you'd still be out on the beat harassing gays,' Clay said, peeved by the officers' poor knowledge of art history.

Ignoring Clay, Detective Walsh picked his way between the easel and a workbench to enter the living space. S.C. Parker hung back. The detective paused by the garage sale three-piece suite to pick up the black silk Japanese smoking jacket that Pamela wore between posing sessions. He slid the silk garment between his fingers and examined the label.

Clay turned to watch the detective and noticed Pamela's neatly folded pile of clothes on the adjacent lounge chair. Pamela hadn't responded to his calling from outside, and now she wasn't responding to their presence inside. Clay glanced up at the loft again. Pam must be up there zonked out on weed, Clay thought.

'These pictures, they're of the same girl as in the painting?' Senior Constable Parker asked from behind Clay. Clay turned to answer; Parker was leafing through a pile of drawings on his drawing table.

'Yes, that's Pamela Moray.'

'The person you were calling for, out front?'

'The same,' Clay replied, spotting his wallet and keys beside the drawings on the same table.

'So where is this, Pamela Moray?' Walsh asked.

'I dunno. I thought she was here,' Clay said.

'Doesn't look like she's here,' Walsh said, moving past a utilitarian kitchen bench containing a sink filled with dirty dishes, paint-stained rags and brushes, toward the red loft ladder.

'I guess not.' Clay turned to face the detective, now worried about Pamela's occasional Hooch smoking.

Becoming impatient with the pointless ping-pong questioning, Clay moved over to the drawing table and picked up his wallet.

'Look, here's my wallet,' Clay said, pulling his cancelled driver's licence out and holding the photo ID up beside his face for them. 'Thanks for the help breaking in, but I'm sure you have more important things to do. Real work, like actual crimes to solve, that sort of thing.'

Walsh paused at the foot of the loft ladder, placed a hand on the side rail, looked up, and then turned back towards Clay.

'Ok Mr. Weston, we'll leave you to whatever it is you do here. I'd think about installing a better front door lock. The one you have is a joke.' Eying Constable Parker, he added, 'Come on, let's go before you turn all artsy on me and want to strip off and go for a wander in the rain.'

'Sounds like a sexist remark, Bill.'

'Report me when we get back to Church Street. You want to grab a coffee on the way, Jen?' The street door slamming shut silenced their banter.

Clay turned, walked over and climbed the loft ladder. Both loft beds were empty. The police presence had sobered him somewhat, but his champagne euphoria had morphed into an afterglow of tiredness that didn't allow him to comprehend Pamela's absence or explain why she'd left her clothes behind. Surely, she'd not left the studio as naked as Young and Jackson's Chloe. Clay dropped onto his bunk, lay back and closed his eyes trying to remember what Pamela had said when he'd left for the gallery party, and promptly fell asleep.

Chapter Two

Incessant knocking on the studio door interrupted ten hours of deep sleep. Clay's head throbbed with a hangover and his thinking exhibited a slowness reserved for snails. Clay massaged his temples a little before pulling on some clean jeans, sandals and a T-shirt and slipped down the loft ladder to answer the door. The knocking stopped before Clay arrived, so the opened door framed empty space. Clay stepped out and looked up and down Cotton Lane. The only person who could have knocked was a slim young woman walking toward Cubitt Street.

'Did you knock?' Clay called.

The girl stopped and turned. Clay watched her long jet-black hair fan out to catch the late morning sunlight streaming into Cotton Lane. The girl walked back along the now dry footpath toward him with a determined mini-skirted sashay, a red patent leather shoulder bag over her left shoulder. Up close, Clay noticed a braided, red-dyed ribbon of hair amidst her black tresses and a wisp of some exotic scent. This is someone I'd like to get to know, Clay thought.

'I would have rung, but you're not listed,' the girl said with a touch of chagrin. 'Are you Clay Weston?'

I am,' Clay said, noting the symmetry of her features and the pleasant cut of her white blouse. 'I don't have the phone connected. How can I help?'

'Typical artist!'

Clay smirked at the remark and turned away, a little disappointed by the girl's attitude.

'I'm looking for Pamela,' the girl said, grabbing his shoulder. 'I believe, she does... nude modelling for you.' The girl withdrew her hand and glanced from side to side as if a little embarrassed by her action or the question.

'Pamela's not here.' Clay answered casually, turning to face her.

'She must be,' the girl insisted, fixing him with an anxious pair of green eyes.' Her Bambino is parked round the corner in Little Cotton Way. Yesterday, before I left for work, Pam told me that she was modelling for you, and she hasn't come home.'

Clay scratched at his two-day stubble giving an impression of thinking but gave a couldn't-care shrug.

'I'm worried,' the girl said, examining her black painted nails. 'Pam missed an important appointment today, and it's not like her to renege on an arrangement.

We both had interviews for a well-paid fashion shoot earlier this morning.'

The girl stopped fidgeting with her nails, and with a stiffening intake of breath looked up at Clay with deliberation, 'I told Pam nude modelling was a bit iffy, but she just laughed at me, her being an ex-art student and all.'

Clay raised an eyebrow.

'Pam told me she'd modelled at art school, and that you were supposed to be a respected artist with gallery representation; whatever that means. So, Mr. Weston, what do you think could have happened to her?'

'I have no idea, but as well as her car, Pamela left all her clobber behind which is unusual. But yesterday and today have been rather unusual.'

'Pam left the clothes she arrived in?' the girl asked, surprised.

Clay nodded.

'Then Pam must still be here. Maybe I should look Mr. Weston,'

The girl stepped around Clay and in through the open studio doorway.

'Call me Clay,' Clay said, following her. 'And your name is?' The girl ignored his question, so Clay trailed in behind her.

Clay's intruder propped just inside the studio door as if having second thoughts about barging in. Clay almost ran into her.

'You live here?' the girl asked, eyes panning left and right.

'I know, I know, Clay said, backing away to an acceptable distance. 'It stinks of linseed oil —'

'— And gum turps,' the girl said taking a gentle sniff. 'I quite like the aroma, a distillate of pine tree resin. I used to work in perfumery.'

'Really, I get taunted so much about the smell.'

'Is that so? I'd have thought you'd get more grief over the mess. My God, look at that floor!'

'Huh.' Clay peered over her shoulder. 'It's a workshop, my painting studio. Not a patch on Frances Bacon's mess yet.' Clay paused to chuckle at his own joke, however when he saw no reaction from the girl, he added, 'And they say, "he who makes no mess makes noth —"'

'— Do they? And Bacon stands for pig, does it?' The girl stepped forward gingerly negotiating the empty paint tins, exhausted oil tubes, buckets of soaking brushes, oil rags, hand towels and takeaway litter.

'Pamela's stuff is on the couch, over there.' Clay pointed past the easels.

The girl nodded but stopped in front of the painting Detective Walsh had uncovered.

'Not bad,' the girl said leaning in for a closer look, 'I can actually recognise Pam.' Clay winced at the comment but chose not to respond. Instead, Clay moved over to the couch to sort through Pamela's clothes.

Jeans, blue with colourful cotton embroidered pockets, white cheesecloth top, bra, panties and Indian style strap sandals. Under everything he found her bag. Clay looked up with a confused expression as the girl joined him.

'Strange,' Clay said, pulling out Pamela's wallet. 'I can't imagine Pamela leaving without her bag and wallet even if she left stark naked.'

Clay threw the bag and wallet back onto the couch.

The girl looked askance at him.

'Not likely. Maybe she had another change of clothes or borrowed some of yours.'

'Anything's possible,' Clay said, remembering the previous night's chaos. The girl looked at Clay as if he was nuts. 'Last night I returned to Cotton Lane in the pouring rain from a gallery after party half cut, half naked and minus my shoulder satchel, keys and wallet, which I must have forgotten when I rushed out. Although I still can't find my satchel.'

The girl still looked at him as if expecting an explanation. Clay shrugged and sagged onto the couch beside Pam's things massaging his temples as if trying to squeeze out a justification.

'Maybe Pam forgot her bag and wallet the way I did,' Clay offered unconvincingly.

'Your experience sounds like the aftermath of being wasted on drink, drugs or both. You artist types might be into that sort of thing, but I know Pam isn't. Pam didn't smoke, except for the odd joint and had only an occasional social drink, nothing excessive. And hear this, mister famous artist, never ever touched hard drugs.'

Clay looked up to see the girl glaring down at him, hands on hips.

'You're her employer,' the girl said in a quiet yet determined voice. 'You're responsible. If you can't or won't find out what's happened to her, I'll call the police.'

Clay's jaw dropped. He rose slowly to his feet.

'Let's not do anything rash,' Clay said, spreading his hands palm up in a conciliatory gesture. 'I'm sure we can figure this out.'

'Well, I'm waiting.' Her voice loaded with scepticism.

'Right!' Clay clapped his hands together and looked at the couch. 'OK. It seems Pam left here, on foot, with no clothes or personal effects, and I'm sure she wouldn't do that without a very good reason —'

'— And your headache suggests drugging,' the girl cut in.

'Maybe. But I can assure you, I don't match your colourful artists' stereotype regarding drugs, so there's probably another explanation.' Clay pointed at Pam's clothes with an imploring gesture. 'Perhaps there's a clue amongst her things.'

Clay stood back and watched the girl perch on the couch to search through Pamela's belongings. Clay noticed her delicate fingers pick through the contents of Pamela's wallet. Clay liked the way she sat with balance, with a model's poise. Clay also noticed her black mini skirt ride up to show considerable thigh.

'I can't find anything that might help,' the girl said, glancing up and catching him staring at her.

'Having a nice perv, are we?'

'Ah. No, not really.' Clay looked down, pretending to focus on Pamela's clothes. Clay bent and picked up Pamela's jeans and started searching the pockets. 'So, no diary or appointment book here.'

'No, Mr. Weston, no juicy diary for you to —'

'Hang on, what's this?' Clay said, thankful for the distraction. Clay waved a business card he'd pulled from one of the pockets. Clay read from the card.

'B.S. Fine Art, National and International Art Valuation, Conservation and Investment Services, Oxford Street, South Yarra.'

The girl stood and with the same fluid movement, snatched the card from Clay's hand. Waving it in his face she said, 'Why would Pam have this in her pocket? She's not into collecting art.' The girl looked hard into Clay's eyes. 'Pam must have picked it up from amongst this mess,' waving the card to encompass his studio space. 'My guess is you, being an artist, it must be connected with this place.'

'Sorry, no, I've never heard of the place. I wonder what the B.S. stands for?'

'Bull shit probably! If you have anything to do with it.' The girl threw the card in his face.

'I'm sorry. As Van Gogh is my witness, I honestly have no idea what happened to Pamela, and I've never heard of B.S. Fine Art.' Clay took a deep breath. 'But Oxford Street; isn't that far from here, I think it's off Chapel Street just down from Toorak Road.'

Clay retrieved the business card from the floor and saw the name Barry scrawled across the back.

'This card was in her jeans pocket, which means it's a place she visited recently. It's possible this Barry may know something. Maybe we should pay them a visit. What do you think?'

The girl rolled her eyes.

'Frankly, I think you're clutching at straws and working hard to get me off your back. It's a dumb idea. I'm more inclined to call in the police and have them search this pigsty for body parts.'

The girl remained attractive despite her anger and Clay still didn't know her name yet. But Clay also knew she was right. Clay was working hard to distance himself from Pamela's disappearance, and he certainly didn't want the police, who already thought he was dodgy, poking around in his studio and jumping to conclusions.

'Look,' Clay said, 'search my place yourself if you like. But think about this. Would I have let you walk in so easily if I had a body tucked away in the loft? I'm as mystified by Pamela's disappearance as you.' Clay almost dropped to his knees. 'Why don't we check this B.S. Art place out together? What have we got to lose?'

'I don't have anything to lose,' the girl said. 'But you sure as hell do. Because if I don't find Pamela, I'm going to report her as missing, last seen in your grot.'

Clay sagged back onto the couch head down.

The girl headed for the reception room entrance, stopped at the doorway and glared back over her shoulder at Clay.

'Well, what are you waiting for? Are we going to check out this place or not?'

'Oh, so now I'm supposed to drop everything and help someone I don't even know.'

'I'm Karen, Pamela's best friend, that's all you need to know.'

Clay jumped up from the couch and followed Karen out, with a smile spreading across his face.

Chapter Three

Clay and Karen caught an empty midday train from Richmond Station and travelled the one stop down to South Yarra, boarded a connecting tram along Toorak Road to Chapel Street, from where they walked the block down to Oxford Street.

A two-storey brick and cement-rendered building housed B.S. Fine Art, which was tucked in between a Trend Furniture showroom and a wholesale Persian carpet distributor. The freshly painted maroon exterior featured cream trompe l'oeil painted Roman columns on either side of a heavy black panel door with the name B.S. Fine Art in polished brass letters across the top third of the door. To the left of the entrance, a shallow display window backed with a heavy red velvet drape featured a single, black-painted timber easel, upon which sat a gilt-framed painting of an outback scene featuring an aboriginal child. Clay recognised the warm earthy tones and subject of an early Russell

Drysdale. The alienated face of the portrait stared into the questioning gaze of Clay and Karen.

Clay took a few steps back and looked at the building.

'Has to be a recent addition to the gallery circuit,' Clay said looking at the other facades up and down the street.

'Why's that?' Karen replied, stepping up to the entrance and waiting impatiently for Clay.

'Because in the fifteen years I've painted professionally, I've sussed out every gallery and art-related business in South Yarra and I don't remember this one.'

Karen tried the large, polished brass door handle.

'Locked! What a waste of time, I should have gone straight to the police.'

'Hang on,' Clay said, joining her at the entrance. After a quick scan of the doorjamb, he found and pressed a small unobtrusive button. 'A lot of these places are only open by appointment.'

'Seems you're not completely useless,' Karen said, stepping back to watch and impatiently tap her foot.

After a second continuous button press, they heard approaching footsteps. A bolt was pulled, and the door swung open enough to allow a cloud of cigarette smoke to escape. A man with small narrow lips and close-set eyes on either side of a crooked nose appeared from behind the smoke.

'Have you an appointment?' he asked, with a rasping nasal twang.

'Not exactly,' Clay said, showing the business card. 'A friend gave us this.'

The man did not reply and made no attempt to open the door wider.

'There are no business hours on your card,' Clay said. 'Only a phone number.'

The man squinted at Clay and frowned with a knowing expression. Clay winced, he realised he'd snookered himself by mentioning the phone number. He'd need more than the business card to get past this guy.

The man moved to close the door, but Clay jumped forward and jammed his foot in the opening.

'Look,' he said. 'We recently obtained access to a valuable collection that we need valued. We could ring and make an appointment, but we're pressed for time. We might have to take the collection elsewhere if —'

The man glared at Clay's foot but eased back on the door.

'— How valuable?'

'Very.'

'How very?'

'Six figures, at least.' Clay turned to Karen for support. 'Wouldn't you say Karen?' Karen looked bored.

'I guess,' she said looking back up toward Chapel Street as if ready to walk.

'All right,' the man said with a steely look. 'I'll give you five. But you better not be wasting my time.'

'We won't,' Clay said, beaming his widest smile at the man.

The man opened the door and stepped back to reveal his diminutive build. He also revealed an imitation leather coat over a black shirt and red bow tie. Clay thought the man looked like a spiced-up jockey.

Clay and Karen entered a rather gloomy rectangular showroom with grey-green walls. The colour reminded Clay of Elephants Breath; a drab colour obtained by mixing all the leftover colours on a palette. Centred in the rear wall, a partially open door led to what Clay presumed was an office or storeroom. A dozen widely spaced paintings by iconic Australian artists covered the walls, each illuminated by individual overhead tracked spotlights.

'Are you Barry?' Clay asked, pointing to the name scrawled across the back of the card he'd retrieved from Pamela's jeans pocket.

'No. Terry Mullet, at your service,' the man said, with an offhand flourish. Mullet walked across the room and flicked his depleted cigarette into a shallow terracotta pot filled with sand. He turned to face them and pulled a fresh pack from an inside pocket, returned, and held the pack out at arm's length to offer them both a cigarette.

Clay and Karen both declined and as Mullet pulled a fresh cigarette from the pack, Karen smiled sweetly and said, 'Actually, I wanted to ask you whether you've seen my friend Pamela?'

Mullet did not react; his expression remained phlegmatic. Instead, he focused on Clay, lit up and inhaled into his scrawny chest. As smoke drizzled from between crooked yellow teeth he squinted at Clay.

'Do I know you?'

'I'm Clay Weston. I'm an artist and this is Karen —' Clay looked to Karen, but she didn't offer her surname. Instead, she stared at Mullet, her smile fading.

'I must 'ave seen your face in the paper or something, eh?'

'Probably, I exhibit at the Blakely Gallery.'

'Yeah, that's probably it,' Mullet said, with a nod. 'Now, tell me about this collection you want valued.'

Clay gazed up at the ceiling, his mind working hard to concoct a suitable story for the non-existent collection he'd conjured. As the pause became telling, Clay turned on his heels and waved his arm to encompass the paintings surrounding them.

'A collection of works, umm, similar to these.'

'Can you be more specific?' Mullet probed, continuing to ignore Karen who paced on the spot and looked desperate to interrupt.

'Well. Let's see. It was a deceased estate.' Clay paused and cast around the room searching for inspiration. He looked at Karen. 'Grandparent of Karen died,' he said, pausing for further inspiration. 'And ah, left her with a house full of paintings. She needs them valued for, um, a probable sale.'

Karen stared at Clay in surprise, but she gave a slightly delayed nod of affirmation combined with a feeble smile.

Clay grinned and continued.

'From memory, the collection consists of a few Heidelberg School paintings along with some early Melbourne and Sydney Moderns.' As Clay strung out the description of the imaginary collection, he drifted across the room toward a wall of paintings, hoping that Karen, whom he could see was still edgy, might jump in and take the lead.

Mullet tracked Clay across the gallery floor, but when Mullet started to follow, Karen grabbed him by his coat sleeve.

'Mr. Mullet,' she implored. 'Are you sure you haven't seen my friend Pamela Moray?'

Mullet brushed Karen's hand from his sleeve, scattering ash, and rebuffing her question by exhaling cigarette smoke towards her.

'Look,' Karen said becoming exasperated. 'I have a picture of her.' She opened her shoulder bag, retrieved her wallet and opened it, to display a photograph in a plastic-covered flap. Mullet took a deep drag on his smoke, glanced at the photo and shook his head.

Karen persisted. 'We know she was here. We found your business card with Barry's name on the back among her things. How do you account for that?'

Mullet slithered into Karen's personal space and breathing smoke through clenched teeth said, 'Listen girly, as I told yur friend, Barry's not me name. Second, I don't 'ave to account for nothin'. Anyone could have written that name on that card, an' finally, I've never seen the woman.' He remained at an intimidating distance.

Meanwhile, Clay had arrived at a painting that looked like a typical Eaglemont landscape. The painting was signed lower right, Arthur Streeton. But it did not remind Clay of any Streeton he could remember. The paint looked very fresh. At first, Clay assumed it had been recently cleaned, but something about the work niggled. The visual patina, the yellowing, the cracking and the accumulated deep grime were what Clay would expect. But it literally didn't smell right. A painting from the 1880s shouldn't smell of oil, which it did, as did the one beside it. Clay figured that something was on the nose here.

'I think you're lying!' Karen suddenly squealed, swinging an arm up to dispel a cloud of cigarette smoke and push Mullet away. 'Pamela's missing!' Karen shouted. 'And if I can't find her soon, I'm going to the police.'

Surprised by Karen's sudden outburst and push, Mullet staggered back almost losing his balance, though he quickly recovered, his face stiffening into a scowl. Mullet stepped towards Karen and drew back his arm to deliver a backhand. It was clear Mullet was not going to tolerate being pushed around by this young woman.

Karen turned away, her left eye remaining focused on the looming slap.

'What the fu-' Mullet grunted with unexpected effort, his hand frozen, unable to move, restrained in mid-air by the wrist.

'I don't think you want to do that pal,' Clay said, adjusting his grip on Mullet's wrist. With a quick twist, Clay swung Mullet away from Karen as if he was weightless. This time Mullet did lose his footing. He fell hard, flat on his backside and slid across the tiled floor, further shining the seat of his pinstripe trousers.

Clay had strength, weight, and height over Mullet. Mullet could see that, so he remained on the floor, his neck veins pulsing with rage. Mullet snarled under his breath and reached inside his jacket. Clay suspected Mullet wasn't reaching for smokes this time.

Karen paled with wide-eyed shock at what this ugly little man on the floor might reveal. She'd seen enough old crime movies to recognise the move.

Clay took a deep breath. The distance to Mullet was too great to land an effective kick in time. If Mullet pulled out something other than smokes, they were in real trouble.

'Terry. Terry, my good man. What are you doing? I thought we had the floor polished a few days ago.'

Surprised, Clay turned to see a man of similar height to him. Standing at least six foot two and dressed in a similar black suit to Mullet's, but of a better cut and fit. Mullet looked up startled as if he'd been caught with his hand in someone else's jacket pocket.

The big man must have emerged from behind the door at the rear of the gallery, Clay thought. He must have been listening back there, in what Clay had assumed was an office. The big man stepped forward and grasped Mullet under one armpit, lifted him into the air and dropped him back onto his feet, then straightened Mullet's bow tie and dusted some imaginary lint from his jacket lapel. Mullet retrieved his hand from his inside pocket in response to a look from his boss that would have sliced through steel. Mullet retreated into the shade of the big guy, who turned to Clay and Karen.

'Name's Barry Scarlet,' he said with a smooth, lightly European accented voice. 'I own this business, and I'm sure Terry, our manager here, has helped you all he can, Mr. Weston.' Scarlet turned to Karen. 'I'm sorry you have lost your friend, but I can assure you we have not seen or heard of the lady. I'm afraid we are currently rather busy and are unable to provide unsolicited valuations at present. Perhaps you could mail us the details of your collection with some appropriate Polaroids. If we can find the time in the next few weeks, we will do an evaluation and get back to you.'

Clay nodded.

'I think our business is concluded Mr. Weston. Terry will see you out.'

Clay nodded again even more effusively.

'Come on Karen,' Clay said, reaching out to take Karen's hand that hung pale and limp by her side.

'Terry!' snapped Scarlet.

'Yes, Boss.'

Following orders, Mullet moved to the door and opened it. Clay guided Karen to the exit, and out into Oxford Street. The door slammed firmly behind them, and they heard the scrape of the bolt being replaced as Clay led Karen towards the relative safety of a busy lunchtime Chapel Street.

Chapter Four

Clay shepherded Karen into the Tre Polli. A small Italian cafe in Chapel Street, two minutes' walk south of Oxford Street. The walk returned some colour to Karen's cheeks, but she hadn't spoken a word since they left B.S. Fine Art.

Clay selected a table for two near the rear of the cafe. He was disappointed with the way Karen had tackled Mullet. They'd not gleaned one jot of useful information on Pamela's possible whereabouts. Karen still looked shaken, so he decided not to mention her aggressive approach to Mullet.

Karen gazed blankly at the mosaic of artworks, including a couple of Clay's own drawings decorating the walls. Clay often visited the Tre Polli for lunch or coffee; it was his favourite Italian cafe. The proprietors, Rosa and Giovanni Lombardi supported artists as only cultured Europeans could. Many local artists met there to talk shop while feeding their caffeine addictions.

'Did you see the size of Scarlet? I'm glad you didn't decide to get physical with him,' Clay said, realising he'd forgotten his previous decision to not mention her crude approach. Clay covered with a nervous laugh.

Despite Clay's ill-considered joke, Karen remained subdued, she continued to stare at the art-covered walls. That bastard Mullet has traumatised her, Clay thought, but he did find Karen's sudden vulnerability appealing. Clay felt his masculine protective urge stir.

'Can I buy you lunch?' Clay suggested, trying to engage Karen. She turned from the paintings and looked at him as if he was a stranger. He supposed he was. Despite what they'd just experienced, they had only met that morning. He still didn't know her full name, something he badly wanted to remedy.

'Lunch! I don't often bother with lunch,' Karen said weakly.

'Rosa makes a delicious prosciutto, ricotta and red-onion marmalade open sandwich. It's only a light meal. I can guarantee that you'll feel better after Rosa's food and excellent coffee.' Clay paused for an answer he did not receive. 'What do you say Karen?' Clay asked again, reaching across the table to touch Karen's hand that he discovered was icy cold.

'I guess,' Karen said, with a faint nod.

Glad to get a response, Clay stood and approached the counter to place an order with the proprietor, Giovanni.

Moustached and round-faced with a permanent jovial expression; Giovanni's ample frame was wrapped in a red and white striped apron. Giovanni oozed Calabria.

'Bella ragazza, Clay,' Giovanni said with a wink. 'I've not seen you in here with her before. She makes the art on my walls pale.'

Clay smiled and ordered two prosciutto sandwiches and two cappuccinos. Giovanni relayed the order over his shoulder to his partner Rosa and turned back to steal another glance at Karen.

'Hey, Giovanni.' Clay said trying to draw Giovanni's attention. 'What do you know about that new gallery in Oxford Street?'

'Not so much mate, except that it has only been there for about three or four months. The owner, he thinks he's some kind of Italian bigshot. Reminds me why I left Italia'

'How's that?'

'Well... he come in here about two months ago, and he ask if we can cater for twenty people. An exhibition opening. Rosa, she prepared her 'chicken with olives'. You know the dish Clay. It's a roasted chicken breast with handfuls of tasty cherry tomatoes, olives, garlic and rosemary. Everything drizzled with genuine Italian olive oil and seasoned with salt and pepper. It's magnifico, eh?' Giovanni paused for Clay's nod of agreement before continuing. 'But when we deliver, he won't pay. Rosa and me, we're still trying to get all the money.'

'He didn't pay?' Clay said, raising an eyebrow.

Giovanni rested two fat arms on the counter, leaned forward and dropped his voice to a whisper.

'I reckon he's a bloody Mafioso.'

'Why?'

'He want an invoice.'

'Oh! Is that all?'

'Sometimes, when we ring about the money, he send that skinny chimney around who work for him, with a few lousy dollar. What's his name? It a kind of fish.'

'Mullet,' Clay offered.

'Yeah, slimy mullet that's it. Real fishy.'

Rosa reached around Giovanni's wide striped apron to place two dishes on the counter.

'Since you still parlando con Giovanni, can you take these two dishes over to your pretty friend, eh Clay? I'll bring your cappuccinos, un minuto'

'Thanks, Rosa.'

Clay ferried their meals over to where Karen sat waiting. Karen poked at her sandwich with such obvious disinterest that Clay thought he'd wasted his time ordering for her. Clay bit into his sandwich and issued a couple of fervent grunts. Clay soon saw Karen's nose twitch from the aroma and after a minute, she picked up half a sandwich and took a bite. Karen's eyes widened.

'Mmmm. This does taste good.' Karen said, taking a second more eager bite.

'I told you,' Clay said, glad of the response.

'I asked Giovanni about B.S. Fine Art,' Clay said, feeling more confident he could now engage Karen in conversation. 'He's also had an unpleasant experience with our friends in Oxford Street.'

Karen stopped eating and frowned at Clay. 'They're not friends of mine,' Karen said, with renewed colour and vigour. 'I'm not surprised. That little runt with the yellow teeth is disgusting! They're liars! How the hell did Pam get that card with Barry's name written on it without having met him? Going there was such a waste of time Mr. Weston.'

'Can't you at least call me Clay, now that I've rescued you from assault and we've shared lunch?' Clay asked, between mouthfuls.

Karen pouted and took another hearty bite from her sandwich.

'Our visit to B.S. Fine Art wasn't a complete waste of time,' Clay said, finishing off his sandwich. 'While you were facing off with Mullet, I had a quick look at a few of the paintings. I'm almost certain they're dodgy.'

'What do you mean?' Karen asked, eyes widening.

'They're fakes, forgeries, that's what I mean. One of the landscapes I looked at was signed with an Arthur Streeton signature. He's a Heidelberg artist from the last Century. The original had to be painted in or around Eaglemont in about 1880.'

'You see Karen,' Clay said, pointing to the paintings hanging on the cafe wall to emphasise his point. 'The paintings at B.S. Fine Art are different, they have the surface appearance of age, but the patina is artificial, created with fresh paint and that paint still retains the smell of linseed oil. There would be no oil smell from a canvas painted over one hundred years ago.'

Karen's eyebrow lifted in amazement.

'How could they get away with that? Surely the painting is documented everywhere. Art books, cata-logues, you name it. If a copy popped up for sale, surely alarm bells would go off?'

Rosa arrived with their coffees.

'Here's your cappuccinos. Also, a piece of my choco-late slice, just baked,' Rosa said beaming at Karen. 'You must have it with your coffee; it will put a little extra flesh on you, eh? Help keep this man interested.'

Rosa wagged a finger at Clay and continued. 'He is like a bee that flits from one flower to another. I see him with so many young —'

Karen giggled over the rim of her coffee mug.

'— Thanks Rosa,' Clay cut in, with an injured ex-pression. Clay tried to pick up the thread.

'Now, where was I... oh yeah. Alarm bells. Not in this case. The painting is not a copy. It's a pastiche, an assortment of picture fragments taken from similar works. In effect, it becomes a new painting, which someone with a rudimentary knowledge might attribute to Streeton. No doubt they claim it's an undiscovered or lost work; new to the market.'

'I see,' said Karen, examining Clay with interest as she sipped her coffee.

'See what?' Clay said his thoughts derailed by Karen's stare.

'I understand about the paintings. I do,' Karen added. 'But it doesn't help me get any closer to finding Pamela.' Karen drained her cup and placed it on the saucer.

'I think,' Karen said with a grave expression, 'I need to report her missing. I don't know what connection Pam may have with this B.S. Fine Art. But if they are as crooked as you suggest, then it makes reporting Pam's disappearance all the more imperati —'

'Before you go contacting the police Karen, let me try some more digging. I'm sure that gallery and Pamela's disappearance are connected. I'll ask around. Someone may have seen Pamela at one of their openings.'

'But Clay, I'm not sure I should wait.'

'Please Karen; just give me the rest of the day. I'll make enquiries. If you give me your phone number, I promise I'll ring you tomorrow. If I don't find her or get any leads, I'll go to the police with you myself.'

Karen grimaced but agreed. She wrote her name and number onto her napkin, folded it and passed it across the table to Clay. Their hands touched. Karen's hand felt warm. She gave Clay a wan smile, stood and left.

Giovanni followed the sound of Karen's heels and sighed as the door closed behind her. Clay watched her leave too, then unfolded the paper napkin and smiled.

'Not a complete waste of time, Karen Bunting, phone 85953405,' Clay mouthed to himself. He folded the napkin and stuffed it in his pocket as he stood and pushed his seat back into the table. Clay waved to Giovanni and Rosa and left the Tre Polli whistling.

Chapter Five

Clay stepped into Chapel Street. A cool breeze ruffled his flaxen hair and scattered leaves between the urgent lines of lunchtime traffic. Melbourne's erratic autumn weather had replaced the morning's vast blue skies with a shelf of frontal clouds, indicating a weather change blowing in across Port Phillip Bay. A missed opportunity. Clay could have been surfing.

Clay dodged across Chapel Street and caught a northbound tram. A block north of Toorak Road it crossed the three spans of the Church Street Bridge. In the overcast conditions, Clay noticed that the Yarra River looked muddier than usual. After passing Swan Street, the tram entered the Richmond gallery district, an area chosen by clued-in gallery owners, more for rising real-estate values than cultural value. When the tram arrived at Waltham Place, Clay jumped off outside the old Methodist Church on the corner.

The narrow footpath on the southern side of Waltham Place led to the prestigious Blakely Gallery. Clay still marvelled at his luck at being represented by Julia Blakely. They'd met at art school in their early twenties and connected because of their similar privileged backgrounds. Julia was studying Graphic Design, while Clay pretended to study Painting. At the time, art schools were awash with well-heeled young women and, as Rosa had aptly put it, Clay had flitted from flower to flower. Clay soon realised Julia was looking for more than a casual fling, a step too far for him, so their relationship had cooled to an affable, respectful friendship.

Clay held an exhibition in a hired church hall, twelve months after graduating. Not "a proper gallery space," as Julia later informed him. At the time, his choice was not motivated by what was best for his future art career, but by the need to be seen to be doing something useful with his recent art qualification.

The exhibition was low-key, opening with little or minimal publicity. To Clay's surprise, the critics went ape over his ill-considered hastily prepared paintings. A week after opening he'd sold out. After that, every prominent commercial gallery director in Melbourne slummed a path to his studio door. He chose Julia's newly opened Blakely Gallery because she understood him, he liked her, and he knew she wouldn't bullshit him. Julia struck the right tone.

Clay thought it was strange how events had turned out. He had opted to study Art after matriculating with high grades from Geelong Grammar, because he hoped it might piss off H.G. In hindsight he'd made an angry choice. Annoyed with others for planning his life, Clay had jumped in the opposite direction, acted on instinct, and satisfied his immediate desires. 'That's me to a tee,' Clay snickered into the stiffening breeze.

Poor old Harold Garter. Harold was Clay's parents' best friend and personal assistant. After Clay's parents died when he was in his early teens, Harold was appointed the administrator of their trust fund, which was established to support Clay until he came of age.

Harold Garter or H.G. as Clay liked to call him, was well-meaning, but never having married, was unsuited to advising or controlling a rebellious teen; it was like expecting oil paint to dissolve in water. Clay and Harold frequently clashed in the early years of their relationship, but Harold's love and respect for Clay's parents and Clay, combined with his steadfast character and knack for meticulous organisation eventually resulted in mutual respect and admiration between the two men. Harold was the only person Clay completely trusted.

Clay's parents left a considerable fortune after their accident. Harold, along with Clay's aged grandparents, looked after Clay. Also proffering advice were his parents' many busybody business friends from the Melbourne establishment. They all expected Clay to slide into an accounting or business degree, to fulfil his destiny and become CEO of Weston Transport Inc. But Clay preferred to choose his own path in life.

Studying art provided Clay with an out that thwarted the oft-asked question: What was Clay to make of his life? Studying art rendered this an open question. Besides, at the time, Clay remembered thinking that he didn't really want to make anything of his life apart from mastering the perfect wave.

Clay pushed open the heavy timber doors into Blakely Gallery, a converted factory space with plenty of old wool store character. The gallery housed three exhibition spaces of varying sizes with Julia's half-glass walled office to the left of the entrance. Julia could see all visitors as they entered the foyer. Clay saw Julia look up the instant he crossed the threshold. She stood, smiled and waved him into her office.

A confident engaging woman of thirty-four, Julia exuded precision and style. A blonde bob framed a fresh earnest face with restrained, impeccable makeup. Her sharp designer suit accentuated slim perfection. Everything about Julia was mirrored in the efficient neatness of her office.

'Hi, Clay I didn't expect to see you today.' Julia extended her hand in greeting. 'I thought you'd be out catching the swell on Port Phillip Bay this morning.'

'You read my mind, Julia,' Clay said, pulling up a chair to sit in front of her desk. 'I should be, but I've been lumbered with an unexpected responsibility.'

'Responsibility! You?' Julia laughed.

'What! You think I'm irresponsible?'

'Aha!' Julia nodded. 'Now you're reading my mind. So, tell me, Clay, what is this huge responsibility that has loomed up and bitten you on the conscience.'

'It's Pamela.'

'She's your latest model, isn't she?' Julia said, averting her eyes and pretending to straighten the few items on her desk that already had the Zen quality of a Japanese stone garden. 'You haven't gone and got the poor girl preg—'

'No!' Clay said without embarrassment but some indignation. 'She's lost!'

'She's a big girl, Clay.' Julia smiled. 'I'm sure she can sort herself out without your—'

'—No! I mean Pamela is missing.' Clay then gave Julia a quick account of meeting Karen and their efforts to locate Pamela.

'My word, you do seem to get into a pickle when it comes to women!' Julia smirked. 'I'm guessing this Karen is a bit of a looker if she's aroused your tiny sense of responsibility.'

Clay ignored Julia's dig, recognising that the hint of jealousy in her remark stemmed from the embers of their own earlier intimacy. Instead, he pulled the B.S. Fine Art business card from his pocket and flipped it onto Julia's desk.

'I'd like your help. I'd like to tap into your industry knowledge,' Clay said, smiling magnanimously. 'What can you tell me about this Barry Scarlet and B. S. Fine Art?'

Clay imagined the cogs in Julia's graphic designer's mind engage as she picked up and examined the card.

'I've seen this name,' Julia said, looking up as if she might find the memory amongst the exposed rafters that spanned the warehouse space. 'I remember,' Julia said, turning to peruse a neat row of primary-coloured filing cabinets behind her. 'I'm sure I received a promo from them.' Julia ran her hand over the red cabinet, and then past the yellow cabinet, before grabbing the top drawer handle of the last. 'I'm sure they offered a group of Heidelberg paintings for sale,' Julia said, opening the blue drawer and pulling a file from it titled Gallery Promos.

Julia opened the folder on her desk. Clay leant forward till their heads almost touched. Julia flicked through the handbills, letters, leaflets and cuttings while Clay was reminded of Julia's particular subtle perfume. The glossy B.S. Fine Art brochure emerged.

'Here it is!' They both looked up eye to eye and paused for a beat. Julia opened the trifold brochure, which refocused their combined attention.

'Yep, they're the pictures I saw this morning,' Clay said, with a slight frown.

Julia examined the images in the brochure.

'I'm not sure I recognise any of them. They look typical of the Heidelberg period, but I can't place any specific painting,' Julia said, tapping the images in the brochure with a perfectly manicured finger. 'I filed this flyer away, figuring that when I had time, I might try to reference these paintings with a bit of research.'

'No amount of historical research will help,' Clay said, shaking his head. 'I've been nose to canvas with these paintings and they exude forgery.'

Julia gave Clay a look of disbelief.

'I'm not kidding Julia, they're dodgy.' Clay stabbed at the pictures with his finger. 'What about Barry Scarlet, Julia, anything about him? Who is he? Where did he spring from?'

Julia looked perplexed.

'I'm not sure I can help Clay. The gallery only recently came to my attention, because the flyer is toward the front of my folder.' Julia looked a little vexed.

Clay shrugged. 'Oh well, it was a bit of a long shot anyway. I found this guy's card amongst Pamela's things, and I wondered if she'd attended a recent showing, event or something. When Karen and I visited B.S. Fine Art, they claimed they'd never seen her.'

'Pamela could have obtained that card from anyone,' Julia offered, with a knowing look. 'It's not uncommon for a director to write their name on the back of a business card, which only has the gallery's name on the front.'

'Yeah, yeah, I know,' Clay said, nodding. 'When I discovered the paintings were iffy and Scarlet's manager turned out to be a stereotypical criminal lowlife, I became suspicious. I speculated that you might have some dirt on Scarlet. I don't know how, but I thought some background on Scarlet might provide a clue to Pamela's whereabouts.'

'Could be white slavery!' Julia said, feigning shock. 'Pamela could be trussed up in a crate on a plane headed for Saudi Arabia right this minute.' Julia strained to stifle a smile.

'The whole mess would be funny if Karen wasn't threatening to run to the police,' Clay said, with a grimace. 'I've already had one embarrassing run-in with a couple of police officers. I'm not looking forward to another interrogation by those philistines.'

Julia burst into laughter and said, 'Could even be a case of model slavery.' Tears appeared in her eyes. 'Good God, Clay, they might regard your studio as an excuse to lure vulnerable young girls like Pamela into modelling for you.'

Clay ignored Julia's second jibe. He rose to his feet ready to leave.

'I'll ask around.' Julia said, wiping the tears from her cheeks with an elegantly patterned tissue she pulled from the desk drawer beside her. Julia stood and followed Clay out to the entrance. Clay paused, turned and cast an anaemic smile back at Julia.

'Oh, and Clay, don't forget I have the month of October pencilled in on my calendar to show your recent work.'

Clay nodded. He blew Julia an exaggerated kiss as he pushed open the heavy doors and left.

It was mid-afternoon when Clay left the Blakely Gallery. The cold front had passed, and Melbourne's changeable weather had switched from woollen jumper back to open-necked shirt. In the balmier conditions, Clay chose to walk back to his studio. Along the way, Clay indulged in a bit of gallery hopping. Three streets down from Waltham Place, Clay turned east into Gipps Street. Numerous commercial galleries littered both sides of the street and the half-dozen cross streets down to Lennox Street.

Property values must be skyrocketing he thought, as he stood in front of the Contemporary Eclipse Gallery. The gallery stood adjacent to another named BAS, The Bohemian Art Space, which despite its name spon-sored traditional neoclassical paintings. The owners of both knew nothing of Scarlet or his business.

Clay managed to visit a further eight galleries close by, touting various styles. At least three were trying to catch the rising wave of interest in Aboriginal art. One very brave soul in Carrol Street was losing money with a sculpture-only gallery, unlike Julia's gallery, which ran with a sound business model based on diversifica-tion across a clutch of styles and mediums. Clay would not have expected anything less of Julia. Like him, she sprang from a family with a solid business pedigree. Another strong reason why he'd chosen Julia to represent him.

By late afternoon, closing time for most galleries, Clay had not discovered any more about B.S. Fine Art than he'd gleaned from Julia. And, by the time Clay retreated from Romani House in Lennox Street, the last echoing white-walled, varnished pine-floored art whore house with bespangled, red-lipped gypsy owner, Carlotta in hot sales pursuit, he wished he'd decided to squeeze in a few waves.

Clay consoled himself with a flat white in a cafe on Swan Street. He'd discovered nothing about Scarlet's background, nor any connection with Pamela's disappearance. But Carlotta's fanciful fortune-telling sales pitch—If he purchased a painting his future would become a secure chain of benign events guaranteed to result in the meeting of a sexy stranger— made him smile.

A strange calm shrouded Clay as he wandered back along Cubitt Street towards his studio. He'd allowed Karen's paranoid fear over her missing girlfriend to unnerve him. Julia was right. He wasn't responsible for Pamela going missing. She could turn up at any time. Could even be visiting her mother or an old boyfriend. The whole situation was a confection. Carlotta may have made one accurate prediction even if he hadn't made a purchase. Karen was a sexy stranger, and he now had her phone number.

Karen had asked Clay to ring her if he found any leads to Pam's whereabouts. Clay hadn't discovered anything from Julia or from a whole afternoon spent shaking down Richmond's galleries.

Clay had promised to ring Karen, but it was late, and he was hungry and tired. He turned into Cotton Lane conflicted. Could he be bothered walking to the phone box at the far end of Cubitt Street to ring Karen and report nothing, or should he return to Swan Street and find a cafe for a bite to eat? Frustration with the whole missing model goose chase won out. He turned on his heel and headed for Swan Street.

Chapter Six

It was well after nine when Clay returned to his Cotton Lane studio. Clay's confident stride faltered when he approached the ill-lit street door to his studio and discovered the door ajar. Clay tentatively pushed the door fully open and standing to one side he peered into the entry. Nothing seemed out of place.

Clay surmised that when he left with Karen earlier that morning, he must have forgotten to properly pull the door shut. With this self-serving rationalisation providing the barest ripple of assurance, he snaked his way in .and crossed the foyer to push open the inner door, reached into the studio and hit the light switch. The fluorescent tubes flickered into life. If they'd been swinging wildly on their support chains, they would have more aptly illuminated the chaotic scene.

Clay stood stunned anxiously surveying the destruction. His studio was trashed. Easels overturned, the contents of workbenches and tables swept onto the floor, paintings dragged from their storage racks beneath the loft and tossed aside. Even his cosseted couch overturned, its stiff wooden legs pointing skyward like roadkill.

The scene possessed the noiseless presence of a conceptual art installation. Rubbish as art had become art as rubbish. Intuitively, he knew that the perpetrators had left. He was alone amidst the disarray, over which hovered two perplexing questions. Why his place? And what the hell were they looking for?

Clay picked his way through the mess, righting his primary easel, and recovering scattered sketches and media swept from his drawing table. He bent to pick up paint tubes, charcoals and prized brushes and upon standing with his arms loaded he froze. Eyes wide, he sank to his knees to examine what remained of the large Leda and the Swan painting that the police had joked about the previous night. The stretcher lay flat on the floor, the canvas gone, flayed from the timber frame with one of his own trimming knives. The discarded knife thrust deep into the side of the pine stretcher.

'I see you haven't replaced that lock, out front Mr. Weston.' Detective Walsh's question shattered Clay's bewildered stare at the remains of his most recent painting.

'No... No, not yet,' Clay mumbled, looking up to see Detective Walsh and Senior Constable Parker standing just inside the door to his studio, both lacking their usual jovial expressions. 'I haven't had time, and now I'm confronted with this break-in,' Clay said.

'I thought you might be redecorating,' Walsh quipped.

'Very funny, Detective,' Clay said, glaring at Walsh. 'Since you're here, how about you do a spot of investigating and find out who the hell would do this to my place?' Clay stood up to confront Walsh. 'I don't suppose you carry a fucking fingerprint kit in your glovebox alongside that set of lock picks?'

'It's strange that you suggest we do some investigating Mr. Weston, because that's exactly why we're here.'

'Amazing! Stunning response time! You guys are so quick. I've only just discovered this debacle myself. Or have there been other crimes in Cotton Lane that propel you to my door?'

'As it turns out, we're here on another matter.'

'Oh! Another matter. And what might that be?'

'We prefer cooperation to sarcasm,' Walsh said, stepping closer to Clay. 'We're here to investigate the disappearance of a woman, known to you as Pamela Moray; I believe she's your current model. In fact, the same person whom you expected to find here when we helped you gain entry last night.' Detective Walsh paused to scan the disarranged studio, before continuing.

'We'd like to search your place. Show him the warrant, Constable Parker.'

Detective Walsh didn't wait for Clay to respond or view the warrant. He advanced into the studio looking left and right trampling over the mess as he went. Officer Parker held up the warrant for Clay to examine.

Clay stared dumbfounded, as the two officers began to move through his studio. Detective Walsh arrived at the loft ladder, placed one foot on the first rung, paused, turned back towards Clay, and said,

'We were told that you were the last person to see Miss Moray.'

Clay wasn't sure if the detective was making a statement or asking a question.

'Is that what Karen told you? Because if it is, you both know that my model wasn't here last night.'

'We can't disclose our sources, Mr. Weston,' Walsh said climbing the loft ladder. 'But you know full well we didn't do a thorough search yesterday.'

As Detective Walsh climbed to the loft, Constable Parker approached Clay. She dropped the warrant on Clay's drawing table, and as she bent to pick up a scattering of drawings from the floor, she asked,

'Is anything missing?'

Clay shook his head.

'No. Not that I'm aware of.'

Clay chose not to mention the hacked canvas. He didn't feel like cooperating. He was annoyed at their lack of interest in his trashed studio, and the way they were treating him like a criminal. Clay knew he wasn't responsible for Pamela going missing.

'Looks to me like someone wrecked my place out of spite. Maybe they don't like artists,' Clay quipped.

'Could the nude modelling have offended someone, a boyfriend for instance?' Constable Parker probed.

'No.' Clay responded, annoyed at Parker's implication that modelling for an artist was somehow immoral. Disgusted, Clay dumped the armfuls of art equipment he'd earlier lifted from the floor onto his drawing table.

'Nothing up here, no blood or female clobber, nothing,' Detective Walsh called from the loft, unable to conceal his disappointment. Walsh climbed down from the loft, and said,

'It's difficult to find signs of a struggle with everything in such a mess. Obviously, any evidence has been deliberately disturbed.'

'Evidence?' Clay asked, turning towards the loft with surprise.

'Of foul play,' Walsh snapped back.

'Do you still have Miss Moray's belongings?' Senior Constable Parker asked, pointing towards the upturned couch and dropping the drawings she'd retrieved from the floor to add to the scatter on the drawing table.

'I expect Pam's stuff is there somewhere,' Clay said, his gaze panning toward his trashed lounge.

Detective Walsh strode to the couch and pulled it aside, making no attempt to right it.

'Nothing here,' he said, overturning the two remaining lounge chairs to peer beneath them, and poking around amongst the scattered cushions on the floor. Next, he turned to pick through the dirty cutlery in the sink, holding the odd butter knife up to examine the blade against the light, before tossing it.

Clay winced and uttered a squawk of displeasure as each knife clattered to the floor.

Detective Walsh looked at Clay surprised, saying,

'What? The sink hasn't been trashed?'

Clay slowly shook his head in the negative.

Walsh shrugged and threw the last knife back into the sink.

'You haven't told us the truth, Mr. Weston,' Senior Constable Parker said eyeing Clay. 'When I asked if anything was missing, you didn't mention Miss Moray's clothes.'

Not admitting to the missing canvas afforded some discomfort for Clay, which he hoped hadn't shown on his face, but to be accused of not admitting to something he was unaware of was annoying.

'I... I haven't had time to look around,' Clay protested, continuing to look towards the sink to avoid the senior constable's eye. Then realising how this avoidance appeared, he turned to confront the policewoman and said,

'If the bloody door was open all day, Pamela or a boyfriend, anyone, could have come back and grabbed her clothes.' Clay was on a roll. 'It's possible Pam was angry about something. God knows, she or her boyfriend could have come back and trashed my place through spite, or due to some misguided revenge.'

Clay choked off his tirade. He suddenly realised he'd suggested that Pamela might have a reason to trash his place, which was not the case. He knew in his heart; it was not how Pam would behave. Also, he could see that his outburst did little to ruffle either cop's resolute expressions. Jesus! Clay thought, even I have trouble believing the bull I'm blurting. He decided to keep his mouth shut.

Both officers waited for him to say more. Clay kept mum, his lips quivering with the effort. A few seconds passed that seemed like minutes, during which Clay wondered why the person who'd trashed his studio would want Pamela's clothes.

Constable Parker took the initiative again, asking Clay,

'Are you now suggesting that a disgruntled boyfriend could be involved? A few minutes ago, you discounted the idea.'

Clay swallowed hard, annoyed by the Constable's failure to understand that his earlier outburst at the suggestion of a jealous boyfriend, was more an artist's reaction to the public's failure to understand the artist-model relationship. He chose not to launch into a philosophical defence of the practice. These philistines would never understand, and he would end up sounding like a guilty man trying to spin a coverup.

'Could be. But in truth, I really don't know if Pamela had a boyfriend or not,' Clay said, attempting a perplexed expression.

'Right then, Mr. Weston,' Detective Walsh said, grabbing Clay's shoulder with a large coarse hand and spinning Clay to face him.

'Here's what I think. This convenient break-in is the lamest excuse I've ever heard to cover up some kind of deviant sexual game you've been playing with Miss Moray. Physical evidence of your involvement in her disappearance is as thin as paint, but currently mate, you are my number one suspect. Circumstantially, you look as guilty as sin and consequently, I'd advise you not to leave Melbourne. Because if Miss Moray doesn't turn up soon, with clothes on in pristine condition, we will arrest and question you further.'

Walsh indicated to Parker with a nod that they'd finished. As they left, Clay watched them both step over the defaced stretcher that had once contained the painting of Pamela.

'Could you recognise Weston with his chest covered?' Detective Walsh asked Parker as they passed through the entry.

'Christ, Bill, do I detect another sexist comment from you?'

'I should hope so, Jen. Aren't you training to be a detective, Senior Constable?'

Chapter Seven

In the taxi on the way to Tullamarine Airport, Clay didn't give a moment's thought to Detective Walsh's dictate to remain in Melbourne. He knew as certainly as a mark followed a brush stroke, that he had nothing to do with Pamela's disappearance and was sure the police interest in him would evaporate the minute Pamela surfaced. The fact that Pamela hadn't retrieved her beloved pink Bambino and was still missing was a worry, but nothing a couple of days spent with a possible boyfriend or relative couldn't explain.

'Weather Bureau reckons we're in for a bit of rain.' The taxi driver glanced over at Clay's unresponsive face. 'Don't s'pose it'll bother you, seeing you're flying out,' the driver added, turning onto the Tullamarine Freeway, no longer expecting a reply. Clay gave a distracted nod to the driver as he mulled over the events of the previous night.

Clay had failed to contact Karen as promised, and as a result, Karen had followed through with her threat to report Pamela missing. Clay was a little dismayed that she'd chosen to run to the police so quickly, but Clay had to admit that he'd not found out anything that might help locate Pamela. Clay chose not to ring and soothe Karen rather than hunt for a functioning public phone box, late at night in Richmond. Instead, he'd spent the evening doing a quick tidying of his studio before capitulating to sleep.

While tidying his studio worktable Clay found his recent unopened mail. The only letter of consequence was one from Weston Transport Incorporated, requesting his attendance at a quarterly board meeting in Sydney, which he'd completely forgotten about. The envelope contained a Qantas flight voucher. The meeting provided an escape from the missing model morass he felt he was being sucked into, so he took it.

On the flight to Sydney, Clay earnestly read the included report from the Weston Transport Art Education Foundation, one of his pet projects. He smiled, remembering the shock expressed by the board when he'd proposed the idea.

After his parents' accident thrust him onto the board of Weston Transport, Clay initially resented the position. Eventually, he grudgingly decided a minimal involvement on the board was a small price to pay for the considerable income Weston Transport provided.

Clay was aware the other members of the board regarded him as little more than a figurehead, despite his holding the controlling interest. Their deference un-successfully masked their belief that he was only the spoilt indulged son of the late owners, with little practical knowledge of trucking. They believed he would always agree with the senior board members and executives in the company. The board members collectively grimaced at Clay's gentle flexing of power, when after five years on the board, Clay proposed the establishment of an art foundation. An idea that occurred to Clay as his growing success with painting kindled more than a cursory interest in it. Julia also thought the foundation was a source of good publicity.

After very little argument the board acceded to Clay's request and passed his resolution. This small power play reminded the board of the strength of Clay's controlling interest. Now years on, after glowing press supports for the foundation, the board had warmed to his increased involvement and now gave him considerably more respect.

Clay digested the rest of the agenda, read the reports from each department, noted any new company initiatives and jotted a few comments next to each item. He finished his work as the jet approached Sydney and prepared to land.

Clay spotted Harold's bowler hat bobbing above the waiting crowd the moment he entered the Kingsford Smith domestic air terminal. At six foot four, Harold was tall for a British migrant born in Liverpool at the outbreak of the Second World War. He looked like he'd just stepped from an episode of "Upstairs Downstairs", spoke with a John Lennon lilt and carried a resume that included a lightly detailed accounting stint with MI5.

'Hello, H.G. I didn't expect you to personally pick me up,' Clay said, dropping his small overnight bag to warmly execute a two-handed greeting.

'A pleasure to be of service Clay,' Harold replied with just the merest suggestion of a bow.

'But I'm glad you did,' Clay added, grabbing his bag and heading for the car park. 'I think I might need your help.'

'I doubt it,' Harold said, following Clay from the terminal. 'The board meeting will present nothing more than the usual fare. I'm sure you're quite capable of handling anything they can throw at you.'

'It's not the board I need help with H.G.,' Clay said, sniffing the humid Sydney air.

Harold propped midway across the car park.

'Not another woman; I really thought you had grown out of —'

Clay stopped and looked back with a pained expression.

'No, not exactly, although a woman is involved, two women in fact.'

Clay related the events of the previous two days as they drove across the Sydney Harbour Bridge towards North Sydney. The Whitely Lavender Bay vista from

The Bridge interrupted his account until they exited and turned onto the Pacific Highway. Five minutes later, Weston Transport's head office facade in Crows Nest, loomed in the Mercedes' windscreen. Clay concluded his account of the wrecking of his studio and subsequent police visit as they pulled into Weston Transport's basement car park.

Harold nosed the Benz into his marked car space, turned off the ignition, pulled the key and turned towards Clay. 'How exactly can I help?' he asked, concern creasing his normally smooth English complexion.

'Remember a few years back,' Clay said, 'you told me you occasionally engaged a corporate investigator to gather business intelligence?' Harold tapped the side of his nose and winked. 'Well, I'd like you to use your contacts to find out all you can about this character Barry Scarlet and his current business.'

Harold glanced up from making notes in a small black diary he'd pulled from the breast pocket of his tweed suit and said,

'You think he may be involved in your model's disappearance?'

'I'm certain Scarlet's gallery is dodgy, and I suspect he and Mullet lied about not knowing Pamela. I'm not sure, but believe me, whoever messed up my studio wasn't a regular burglar because nothing a thief would want was taken.' Clay said, frowning. 'Someone connected with Pamela broke in because they took only her clothes and my painting of her. They trashed my studio to cover their intentions. In addition, there's the fact it happened directly after I questioned Scarlet.'

'Very well Clay, I'll see what I can turn up,' Harold said, closing his notebook. 'Also, I think we should check out Pamela as well.'

Clay was perplexed but nodded in agreement. He realised Harold was right. They needed to look at both sides of the equation.

'Thanks, H.G. One last thing before we face the board.'

Harold's brow furrowed.

'Can we keep this matter just between us? I'd rather not have the board sweating over this issue.'

'Not a problem, Mr. Weston.'

Clay winced on hearing Harold's salutation but did not admonish him, as he knew his reversion sprang from a genuine concern. They both climbed from the car and walked to the lift, which would take them to the conference room on the top floor.

Chapter Eight

'I knew that poncy painter was iffy,' Detective Walsh said, with a forlorn wave of his hand. 'This poor girl's naked body must have been in the loft that first night we helped him gain entry.' Detective Walsh stepped aside to let a police photographer take a series of evidence shots. Constable Parker frowned at what was presumed to be Pamela's body but responded to Detective Walsh's allegation with a slow shake of her head.

'What?' Detective Walsh stared hard at Senior Constable Parker nonplussed by her reaction, then launched into his justification.

'Weston's not so cute now, is he? We have him cold. The missing girl's body, wrapped in one of his porn paintings, hidden in this industrial waste dumpster not fifty metres from his grot. Probably thought she'd be safely buried under landfill by now. Would have been too, if those kids hadn't skipped school for a bit of dumpster diving.' Walsh glanced towards three subdued yet still fascinated young boys, corralled by a local junior constable a little further down the lane.

'We haven't confirmed that this is the missing girl yet, Bill.'

'Oh, come on, Jen. That pink Fiat Bambino parked over there is registered to Pamela Moray and look at that painting, it's the same one you uncovered on our first visit to his —'

'— Bit obvious dumping the body wrapped in one of his own paintings in the lane outside his studio, don't you think?'

'Bloody oath, it's obvious! The obvious first rule of homicide Parker, suspect the boyfriend. And where is the prick, eh? Gone, scarpered, when I told him to stay put.'

Detective Walsh stretched with a commanding smirk.

'Parker, do you think you can arrange for Karen Bunting to identify this mystery body?'

Constable Parker ignored Walsh's sarcasm but acknowledged the request with a nod, turned, issued a muffled grunt and walked back to their patrol car.

'What was that love?'

'Name's Senior Constable Parker,' Parker said slamming the patrol car door.

Detective Walsh grinned. He joined Constable Parker in the car. In silence, they both watched the forensics team erecting a privacy screen around the dumpster. Detective Walsh broke the silence with a question.

'Any ideas on the cause of death, Senior Constable Parker?'

'Marks about the neck.'

'Which indicates?'

'Possibly strangled, but I'd wait for the post-mortem to confirm.'

'Spot on, Senior Constable Parker,' Detective Walsh said, still gazing at the dumpster. 'And the minute we get back to the station, Senior Constable Parker, I want you to find out all there is to know about our suspect dauber and where the hell he might have gone.'

Walsh paused for almost thirty seconds before adding. 'Jen, I am thinking about the conspicuous nature of the evidence that you noted.'

Constable Parker swallowed a chuckle, started the car and headed for Richmond Police Station.

Chapter Nine

The Weston Transport board meeting required Clay's full attention, to which he tried at feigning involvement, but an underlying sense of impending disaster distracted Clay like an unwanted dribble of paint.

Why had the intruder trashed his studio and taken only Pamela's clothes and the painting of her? Clay couldn't rationalise any of it. Was the trashing simply a malicious act or an attempt to cover the theft of the picture? His suggestion to the police that a disgruntled boyfriend might be behind the break-in fitted the facts but was unlikely, he thought.

The meeting dragged on. The cosseting environment of the conference room and the catered lunch of boutique sandwiches provided little respite from the questions nagging Clay. Soon after 5PM the meeting paused, when Harold Garter entered the boardroom and signalled for Clay to excuse himself. The rest of the board fell silent at Harold's entry and watched bemused as Clay was shepherded from the room.

Harold hurried Clay into a nearby office and carefully closed the door behind them.

'What's up HG? You enjoy this cloak and dagger stuff, don't you?' Clay said, with a spreading grin. 'Have you already found out about Scarlet?'

'No, not yet, we have another problem.'

Harold moved in closer to Clay and lowered his voice.

'Five minutes ago, on the ABC News.'

'What?'

'The police found the body of a naked girl wrapped in a painting in a dumpster in Little Cotton Way. No names yet, but they are saying they want to question an artist. I don't need to be Sherlock Holmes to know who they've found and who they want to question.'

'My God, poor Pamela.' Clay's face blanched and he staggered back groping numbly for a non-existent chair.

Harold caught Clay's elbow for support.

'Clay,' Harold said, searching Clay's face. 'You had nothing to do with this, right?'

'Nothing! I swear.' Clay took a deep breath.

'God, I'm sorry H.G. I'm sorry I dragged you into this mess. When I asked for your help, I had no idea poor Pamela would turn up dead.' Clay buried his face in his palms. 'Honestly H.G. I thought, maybe she'd gone to visit family, or hunkered down with a boyfriend, anything but this. But this looks like she's mixed up in some serious shit,' Clay sagged at the knees. 'What the hell am I going to do?'

Harold tugged at Clay's elbow and said, 'Listen up, Clay. You need to find a bit of spine.' Clay raised his head. 'You can't hang around here waiting for my enquiries to bear fruit either.' Harold lifted Clay erect. 'The police will soon uncover your connection with Weston's Transport. In fact, I'm surprised we haven't already had a call.'

'I'll have to fly back to Melbourne,' Clay murmured, with an aggrieved sigh. 'Someone has painted me right into this dirty picture, and that bloody Detective Walsh already has me sketched in as the bad guy. I need time. Time to prove I'm innocent.' Clay stared fiercely into Harold's eyes. 'Time to prove I've been framed.'

'No! No!' Harold said, waving his hands in front of Clay's face to attract his attention. 'You can't fly, the police will be waiting for you at Tullamarine.'

'I'll hire a car.'

'No good Clay, they will be watching the hire car companies. It's standard procedure.'

'Then I'll hitchhike.'

'No need for that, my boy. I'll arrange for you to catch an overnight ride back on one of our trucks. After all, we are a transport company.' Harold smiled; it was obvious he revelled in the intrigue. 'Because of your alternative, I mean art career, you're not well known around the company except by a few head office staff and of course the board members.' Harold paced to the door and back as he spoke, as if wary of being overheard. 'There's no need to tell the driver who you are. I'll tell him you're a new employee returning to the Melbourne depot. Use the truck's sleeper berth on the way back to Melbourne to avoid conversation and keep out of sight. Don't go near your studio in Richmond, the police will be watching it. And the same goes for any of your regular arty friends. Book into a motel,' Harold said, pulling an envelope from his pocket. 'There is one thousand in cash in this envelope; don't use your credit card.'

Clay was astonished at Harold's command of the situation but grateful that someone was firmly in his corner. The events of the last few days had rattled his usual confidence.

'God, I'm sorry to drag you into this mess, H.G. I'm so relieved you believe me.'

'You might have thrown your life away in the pursuit of art and surfing, but I don't think you're crazy enough to commit murder, even in the name of Art.' Harold said this with such a straight face that Clay was left gaping.

Harold headed for the door. 'I'll organise the driver while you take your leave of the board.' Harold opened the door to leave and paused. 'Make sure you ring me from a public phone when you get settled, by then I might have some intel on B.S. Fine Art, Scarlet and Pamela that might help.' With that said Harold left.

After a moment to regain his composure, Clay returned to the boardroom to make his apologies for having to leave early. Clay was sure the board would feel relieved to have him gone. They made no objection to his departure.

Thirty minutes later at 6:10 PM Clay was safely riding beside driver Russell Baker, in the prime mover of a twenty-two-wheel articulated semi-trailer as they crossed Sydney Harbour Bridge, heading for the Hume Highway.

Chapter Ten

Clay felt uncomfortable having to lie to Russell Baker about who he was and why he needed a ride to Melbourne on one of Weston Transport's overnight haulers. As soon as he could, he excused himself from the small talk by saying he was tired and retired to the truck's sleeping cab not long after they settled into cruising speed on the Hume. The hum of the tyres, the drum of the big 7.6-litre diesel engine and the rock and roll of the cab, did their best to transport Clay into the land of nod, but his mind fidgeted with thoughts of how he could clear himself and where in Melbourne he might safely avoid the police. Eventually, mentally exhausted he slept.

'Wake up, son,' Russell said, reaching back into the sleeping cab to roughly tousle Clay's sleep-set hair. Clay stirred but didn't open his eyes.

'It's 5 AM and we've arrived at the Campbellfield depot.' Russell shook Clay again. 'Crikey mate, I still can't figure out why Sydney head office couldn't organise a flight voucher for you. Would have been a darn site quicker and you wouldn't have arrived looking like shit. You must have crapped heavily on someone's boots for them to withhold a voucher. I'd be talking to the union if I was —'

'— The office?' Clay interjected, poking his head out of the sleeper cab to cut Russell's rant.

Russell pointed silently at a flat-roofed cement-brick building with two softly lit windows on either side of a red door labelled WESTON DEPOT ADMIN. 'That's the place you're after.'

Clay crawled into the driver's cab and focused his sleep-clogged eyes in the direction Russell indicated.

Russell rummaged in the door storage. 'Tell Rosie at reception I'll be in for a coffee with my logbook when I've unhooked this trailer.'

Clay popped the door, climbed down to road level and headed for the office throwing a thank-you gesture over his left shoulder to Russell.

The big diesel roared, and the rig lurched into motion crawling across the gravel yard to a row of loading bays in front of an immense grey sheet-steel warehouse.

Rosie looked up at Clay. She didn't recognise him but readily accepted Harold Garter's signed memo and called a taxi for Clay. Clay left in the taxi just as Russell Baker returned to the office. He watched Clay depart, shaking his head, hands on hips.

'Well, I'll be fucked,' Russell said to Rosie on entering the office. 'Where the hell is that boy off to?'

'Broadmeadows Station after that, I dunno,' Rosie said, with a raised eyebrow. 'Had a memo from Sydney head office saying I should give him whatever he wants.'

'I'll be fu —'

'— That's enough trucker's language, Russ. Give me your logbook. By the time I've recorded your details, my shift'll be over. Fire up the jug if you want to be helpful,' Rosie said, smiling.

* * *

At Broadmeadows Station Clay boarded the 6 AM train to Melbourne. The early bird commuter rush to Melbourne had begun, but Clay was still able to secure a window seat in the rear corner of a carriage. He sat self-absorbed, mulling over his predicament. Harold had advised Clay to remain in Sydney and even suggested he stay in a trusted friend's apartment, but Clay was not one to sit around trimming his nails. Back in Melbourne, he could at least make a start on finding Pamela's murderer. When Clay thought about how he might begin, he soon realised that Pamela was a blank canvas to him, he needed to find out more about her.

Pamela had been his regular life model for about a year, and visually he knew every inch of her. Yet, despite the fact they'd spent many hours together, he knew next to nothing about her. Like many artists,

he suffered from the artist's right brain, left brain di-
chotomy. Whilst concentrating on drawing or painting,
primarily a right brain activity, Clay literally lost the
power of speech, because his speech-controlling left
brain was offline. Painting and drawing sessions with
Pamela were marked by a concentrated silence. In fact,
while Clay painted, Pam often resorted to reading a
paperback during her break between poses.

'For God's sake man!' Clay quietly chided himself.
'You're an artist; you're supposed to be observant.
What have you observed apart from her distribution of
masses?'

Well, he knew that Pam had been an art student because she'd mentioned this when applying for the job.
From her behaviour, Clay inferred that she was reliable
as she was always on time. 'Wow! Look out, Sherlock.'

'What else?' Well, Pam was helpful, because sometimes, when he was consumed by the act of painting
to the point of rudeness, she offered to run errands.
Once, he remembered her offering to help him clean
up his studio, a truly selfless act, in view of its scram-
bled state. Clay had never seen her smoke; she didn't
appear to be on drugs. Add to this truthfulness, po-
liteness, and an even-tempered nature. Clay began to
wonder who the hell could be motivated to murder
such an angel.

'That is...' Clay pondered, addressing his reflection
in the carriage window, 'unless these were the very

character traits that led to her murder. Could her honesty have enticed her into a whistleblowing situation? Maybe she knew something. Some information that someone might regard as dangerous?' Clay stared at his reflection as if expecting an answer. 'Where would I start, to find answers?' Clay mused out loud, his voice rising with excitement.

Suddenly, Clay became aware that other passengers were eyeing his one-sided conversation with amusement. Clay gave them a weak smile, slumped in his seat and turned away to look out the train window at the rush of graffiti sprayed across every available surface along the route. If only the answer to his questions lay in those strange yet fascinating urban hieroglyphics that required a Rosetta stone to decipher.

In that instant Clay realised that Karen Bunting was the key. Thanks to Karen, Clay knew that Pamela occasionally picked up the odd fashion photography-modelling gig to supplement her modest income, which meant she was often on the lookout for work opportunities. Clay needed to question Karen again.

At Flinders Street station Clay boarded a Sandringham line train. As the train passed through Richmond Station he was tempted to return to his studio, but when Clay looked down Cubitt Street from the carriage window, he spotted a police van parked a short distance from his Cotton Lane studio. Harold's warning about police surveillance had proved correct.

The Sandringham line would take him south to Brighton Beach Station, a place Clay was familiar with due to his passion for swimming and his knowledge of the Bayside precincts.

Brighton was one of Melbourne's wealthiest beachside suburbs in which, thanks to Harold Garter's financial acumen, Clay owned several investment properties. Clay knew nothing of the properties, having only seen their addresses and descriptions in investment documents that he'd authorised. He knew that they would most likely be leased and occupied and that he could not use any of them as a safe house. However, one of the quirkiest investments that Harold had arranged for Clay, essentially as a private joke, was the purchase of one of the few remaining Middle Brighton Beach bathing boxes. A fight with the State Labour Government by Brighton residents to preserve the quaint Victorian bathing boxes had erupted in the papers at the same time Harold was acquiring investment properties for Clay. Harold correctly argued that buying a box was a good investment because its value would rise if they were declared as heritage architecture, which proved to be the case. Of all Clay's investments, the brightly painted, timber-framed, weatherboard and corrugated-iron roofed bathing box came to be his most treasured possession despite its lack of electricity or running water. During all seasons and quite often in summer, Clay used his box to sleep on the beach, so it was comfortably equipped with a cot, cane easy chair, a small table and a camping gas ring. The box was a home away from home, a haven where he could relax. Unlike his cluttered studio, the close confines of the box necessitated a Spartan neatness that facilitated clear thinking. Now it would provide Clay with a suitable hideout as well.

On the walk up the foreshore from Brighton Station to his bathing box hideout on Middle Brighton Beach, Clay wondered how he could convince Karen to help him.

Chapter Eleven

After Clay settled into his bathing box hideaway, he walked back along Brighton Beach to the Brighton Beach Hotel for breakfast. At the hotel, he could use the public phone to ring Karen. He still had the paper napkin with Karen's phone number folded in his wallet. It was just after 10 AM when Clay rang. The phone rang on and on for ages, and he was concerned that he may have missed her. He was about to hang up when she answered.

'Hello?' came the sleep-fogged query.

'Hi Karen, it's Clay.' Before she could reply, he added, 'I need your help.'

Clay jumped in fast with the request, because he thought that Karen would hang up as soon as she heard his voice. A long silence followed. Clay wondered if Karen had heard what he said.

'Who?'

'Clay, it's Clay Weston,' he repeated, with still no response from Karen. 'The artist,' Clay added, to clarify.

'The murderer!' Karen gasped, suddenly spluttering awake. 'You bastard, what a nerve you have ringing me! Yesterday, I had to identify Pam's body for the police. I should hang up on you and ring them right now.'

'No, don't do that. Please, Karen, think about it. Would I be ringing you if I'd murdered Pamela?'

'You might. According to the police you're a perverted sex killer. You might want to add me to your list of victims.'

'Yeah, yeah, I'm the killer who saved you from that weasel Mullet and took you out to lunch'—

'—And didn't ring me back when you promised. Left me no choice but to ring the police. And then the next day poor Pam turns up. Dead!' Karen started to sob. 'Wrapped in one of your... your paintings...'

'Exactly Karen! A bit obvious don't you think? Why would I draw attention to myself like that? I'm really sorry I didn't ring. I didn't find out anything useful about Barry Scarlet and B.S. Fine Art, and by the time I got back to my studio to find it trashed and was reinterviewed by the police, it was too late to go looking for a working public phone to ring you. Honestly, I had nothing to do with Pamela's disappearance. I thought she would simply turn up. I was exhausted so I crashed out. When I woke the next day, I discovered I was required to attend a meeting in Sydney, so I took the avoidance option. I left because I was sick of all the police harassment and tired of the whole disruption to my routine.' Clay paused for Karen to respond; hearing nothing he continued. 'But Karen, I came back. I wouldn't have come back if I'd murdered Pamela. I came back to find out who the hell did, and you're the only person who can help me.' Clay again waited for Karen's response but could only hear convulsive breathing. Clay figured his best course of action was to keep talking.

'Listen, Karen, Julia Blakely at Blakely Gallery can confirm that I was at her gallery the night Pamela went missing. I swear, I left Pamela at my studio that night and went straight to the Blakely Gallery for an opening.' Clay paused again. Karen still said nothing, but Clay did hear her breathing ease. Karen either had enough pluck to want to know what happened to her friend or thought that Clay might reveal his whereabouts, which she could then relay to the police.

'How about we meet at Blakely Gallery? It's a public place. Julia can vouch for me, and we can discuss what to do next. What do you think?'

'I'm not sure that meeting you is a good idea. Detective Bill Walsh reckons you're as dodgy as —'

'— Really, well that cop has a pathological dislike of artists.' Clay heard a stifled giggle from Karen.

'Please Karen, I need help —'

'— Yeah, that's what the detective said,' Karen interjected, which a relieved Clay interpreted as a lightening of Karen's mood and tentative agreement to his suggestion.

Clay pressed on in hope. 'I just need some information on Pamela's interests, other jobs and possible movements prior to and when she modelled for me. Something I could follow up on that might explain why she was murdered. And Karen, I promise this time I'll definitely keep you informed.'

'All right Mr. Weston; I suppose I can give you one last chance. I'll meet you at that gallery.'

Clay gushed with relief, 'I can be there, around noon today if that's okay with you?'

'I guess, but I warn you if you are fooling with me, I will not hesitate to dob you in to your detective friend.' Karen hung up.

Clay whistled a sigh of relief as he replaced the phone handpiece.

* * *

Clay arrived at the Blakely Gallery at twenty past twelve. On entering he could see Julia and Karen already chatting in Julia's office. The two women did not notice Clay's arrival. To Clay, they appeared engaged in a convivial conversation which rather ominously ceased the instant Clay entered Julia's office.

'Here he is now,' Julia said, moving quickly from behind her desk to claim Clay's arm and plant a light peck on his cheek. Clay recoiled a little and looked askance at Julia.

'See Karen, he's not dangerous at all. All you need to do is show a little affection and he will cringe like a rabbit caught in a shooter's spotlight.'

Karen chuckled and the two women exchanged knowing glances. Clay wished he'd arrived on time. Obviously, Julia had painted a lurid picture of him for Karen's benefit.

Clay became busy with the only other free chair in the office, positioning it in a non-threatening way, equally distant from both Karen and Julia.

'Clearly, you two have become acquainted,' Clay said, trying to project a nonchalant seriousness. 'Have you told Karen that I was here at the gallery the night Pamela went missing?' Clay looked at Julia with a lets-get-serious look.

'Of course,' Julia said, with a flippant shrug of her shoulders.

Changing tack, Clay asked, 'Have the police visited the gallery?'

'I had a phone call yesterday from a Senior Constable Parker wanting to know if I'd seen you or knew where you might be.'

'What did you tell her?' Clay said, showing some concern.

'I told S.C. Parker that I hadn't seen you and that I manage the sale of your artworks from exhibitions and gallery stock, the same as I do for the other nine artists I represent.' Julia paused to look directly at Clay before adding. 'I made it quite clear that I don't manage your private life.'

'So, you didn't help me? Clay rolled his eyes in exasperation. 'Why didn't you tell Parker I was here at a gallery opening when Pamela went missing?'

'Parker didn't ask,' Julia said, before continuing emphatically. 'At the time, I didn't realise that the Herald-Sun headline — BODY FOUND IN DUMPSTER — referred to Pamela.'

'Great!' Clay said, groaning. 'So, the police still don't know I had nothing to do with this mess.'

Julia bristled at Clay's accusation.

'I think the police were more concerned with finding you. Senior Constable Parker implied by her questions that I might be hiding you. I made it quite clear that I wasn't. Although now that I'm conspiring to help you, I guess I'll be regarded as an accessory.'

Karen leaned forward and tapped Julia's desk to disrupt the intense glare between Clay and Julia.

'Can we dispense with this little domestic and discuss the reason we're here?' Karen asked, pausing for breath 'I know you're only interested in getting the police off your back Clay. But I for one, would really like to find out who killed my friend, because the police sure as hell don't seem to have a clue.'

'That's true,' Clay said, relaxing back into his chair. 'I'm still certain that Pamela has some connection with

Barry Scarlet. There must be some link apart from the business card.'

'Well, maybe I can help,' Julia said, reaching behind her into the blue filing cabinet and removing the flyers folder Clay saw a few days prior. 'Remember this pamphlet I showed you from B.S. Fine Art advertising those Streetons? Well, after your last visit, I noticed this in last month's edition of Art Almanac.' Julia pulled the small A5-sized magazine listing the exhibition schedules for most gallery spaces in Melbourne from the folder. Julia spread the open magazine on her desk for Clay and Karen to see. Below a half-page advertisement promoting the same Streeton paintings Clay had seen at B.S. Fine Art was a listing in small type.

EXHIBITION HOSTESS REQUIRED

B.S. Fine Arts have a position for an elegant young
woman with a sound knowledge of fine art to
act as a customer liaison and sales hostess
at Gallery openings.
Contact B. Scarlet
03 8290 0101

'I wondered,' Julia said, pointing at the advert and looking across at Karen. 'Could Pamela have applied for this position?'

'It's possible,' Karen said, leaning forward to examine the magazine. 'We were both trying to pick up part-time work to supplement our modelling careers. That's why Pam was working for Clay.' Karen shot Clay a reproachful look and in response, Clay straightened in his seat.

'This magazine looks familiar,' Karen said, picking it up to examine it. 'I recognise the cover image. I'm almost certain I saw Pam with a copy. I have no other friends with an interest in art and artists, so I must have seen Pam with it.'

'OK,' Clay said. 'We know Scarlet was looking for a gallery hostess. Pamela may have applied for the job, but it's still a very flimsy connection,' Clay said, his shoulders slumping before adding, 'and Scarlet could still deny any connection. Also, the police would just laugh at this evidence.'

Julia adopted Rodin's thinker pose with her elbow on her desk. After a minute's reflection, she said, 'We need to draw Scarlet out.' Julia glanced at Clay. 'If he is peddling forgeries as you say, Clay, then maybe we could tempt him.'

'Right,' Clay agreed enthusiastically. 'What do you have in mind, Julia?'

'If we could just set him up somehow,' Julia mused.

'I think I have an idea!' Clay jumped to his feet. 'We need to give the police a reason to investigate.' He rubbed his hands together to firm up the idea.

'I could knock up some fakes, which you, Julia, could offer to him as bait, and then all we need to do is arrange for the police to catch him red-handed accepting the forgeries, and his whole dodgy enterprise will collapse under police scrutiny.'

'Sit down, Clay!' Julia stared up at Clay aghast. 'That's a crazy plan! Scarlet might end up in jail, but so would we for forgery and fraud.'

Karen looked at them both, astonished.

'No, no, it's not crazy,' Clay objected, waving his finger in the air. 'Look at the law regarding forgeries. I can copy the work of any artist, as long as I don't apply that artist's signature. We leave that bit to Scarlet. Because Scarlet knows that without the right signature, the painting's not worth a bean.' Clay began to pace about Julia's office like a mad scientist. 'That's the bait.'

'Also, Julia, when you present the paintings to Scarlet, you feign ignorance. You let him invent the authorship and provenance and determine the value. That's his business. It's what he advertises on his business card.' Clay pulled the B.S. Fine Art card from his pocket and slapped it down onto Julia's desk. 'See!'

Julia and Karen both leaned forward to read the inscription on the card. "National and International Art Valuation, Conservation and Investment Services".

With a magician's hand flourish, Clay continued, 'All we have to do is anonymously tip off the fraud squad.'

Julia winced; no doubt worried her business reputation might be in jeopardy if the fakes should be traced back to her.

Karen stared at Clay unconvinced then asked,

'How long would it take you to paint these fakes, Clay?'

'Couple of weeks tops,' Clay said, with a smug smile.'

'A couple of weeks! That's way too long. The trail will be stone cold!' Karen shook her head. 'What if Scarlet doesn't take your so-called bait, then we've wasted two whole weeks.'

Exasperated, Clay said, 'Got a better idea? Scarlet knows us Karen, we can't just turn up at his gallery, he'll figure something's up. Julia is the only one who can approach him.' Clay sat back down unable to hide a rising sulk.

Standing abruptly, Karen mouthed at him, 'Waste of time.'

Julia frowned and said, 'I guess we could try to bait him. I can't think of anything else.'

Disgusted, Karen stormed towards the door, she paused with her hand on the handle, 'It's an utter waste of time, Clay.' She glared at him. 'I don't know why I let you sucker me in again. I only agreed to meet with you because I thought you were too stupid to have murdered poor Pam.' Karen wrenched the door open. 'Make sure you bloody well ring me this time, otherwise I just might change my mind and ring the police again.' Karen slammed the door as she left.

Clay's sulk changed into a sick expression.

Julia looked a little shaky, no doubt still concerned by her role in the ruse.

'Karen's really keen on you Clay,' Julia said with an impudent grin.

* * *

Clay had some fifty-year-old canvases, which he'd purchased at Brown's Richmond Auctions in Bridge Road, stored at his Cotton Lane Studio. He smiled at the memory of Walsh's and Parker's reaction to the stack of paintings they'd seen on entering his dusty reception room. Clay needed an old canvas as a support for his fake painting bait, but he had to avoid his studio, which he presumed was still under police surveillance. He would have to use some painter's tricks to age a fresh canvas and stretcher.

On the way to his Brighton Beach hideout, Clay visited Eckersley's Art Supplies in Commercial Road, Prahran, where he purchased the equipment, he needed to get started.

By mid-afternoon a soft autumn light accompanied by a pleasant bay breeze streamed in over his left shoulder through the open bathing box doors to illuminate the small canvas he'd prepared. Clay gazed at the pristine canvas with a dreamy air of anticipation. Karen was right about the time it would take him to produce a suitable painting. The choice of artist and technique was imperative. Clay knew that most early Melbourne modernist artists worked quickly, alla prima or wet on wet and that this method would produce the quickest result. However, many of those painters were still living or dead, their direct descendants were very much alive and available to verify pictures. Clay recalled the paintings he'd seen at Scarlet's gallery. After some thought, he chose to reproduce a late work by Frederick McCubbin.

Strangely enough, McCubbin lived in Kinane Street off Bay Road, about halfway between Clay's bathing box hideout and Brighton Station for about five years from 1894. Clay knew that McCubbin painted a few Middle Brighton Beach landscapes during that time, and it seemed apt that he take advantage of the milieu he now found himself in. McCubbin's painting style, loosely known as Australian Impressionism relied on palette knives, broad brushwork and rag-wiped strokes. He was known to have experimented with unusual techniques such as using unprimed cotton canvas upon which he sometimes scraped a thin layer of lead white into the weave in order to create the high key colouring needed to capture the strong Australian light.

Clay felt sure he could reproduce a reasonable Mc-Cubbin pastiche, but as his hand hovered over the prepared canvas, he felt a stab of regret at having to use his craft with such insincerity. Did the end justify the means, even if to catch a murderer? Doing nothing was not an option, and he was damned if he was going to languish in his bathing box waiting for the police to arrest him for Pam's murder.

Clay's trepidation was not only confined to the morality of painting a forgery. Karen's attitude to the plan to expose Scarlet also chewed away at his composure. Clay worried about what Karen might do next.

Chapter Twelve

Lost in the act of painting, Clay spent all weekend and Monday savouring the feel of palette knife on canvas. Doing little but paint, swim, eat and sleep.

By Tuesday, after a short early morning run along the beach, Clay returned to his bathing box to scrutinise the almost completed painting. He was pleased with his progress. Clumps of straggly tea tree dominated the middle ground of the composition, between which sandy paths trickled between sprays of spear grass and sedge. At the foot of one tea tree, two children played in the sand, dwarfed by the vastness of the beach. The sky, a pale misty blue, dominated the benign expanse of Port Phillip Bay. Deep in the distance on the bay's horizon, a northerly streak of smoke from a departing steamer implied a balmy northerly. Clay relished the painting's quintessential McCubbiness; he now felt confident he could complete the forgery to the standard required to execute their plan.

The mock McCubbin had progressed to the point where the obsessive allure of painting had weakened enough for Clay to contemplate more prosaic thoughts, such as Karen's threat to ring the police if he didn't keep her informed. At the same time, Clay remembered the need to check in with Harold Garter. Clay hoped that Harold had unearthed some information on Barry Scarlet's fraudulent art dealings, information he hoped he could take to the police. Evidence of criminal behaviour by Scarlet would abrogate the need to complete the forgery, which Clay felt he was enjoying far too much.

Clay changed into a clean pair of jeans and a fresh t-shirt, locked his bathing box and walked up the beach towards the Brighton Beach Hotel for his usual counter breakfast. Pub food, mostly fry-ups were not going to do much for his health, but neither was a stint in gaol, so the food that Red, the barman provided was a necessary inconvenience. Red poured Clay a cup of coffee and handed him the coins he needed to use the hotel's public phone.

Clay dialled Karen's number first. As the ringtone dragged on, Clay imagined Karen's sleepy, baby-doll-attired swagger toward the ringing phone. Clay still hadn't entirely given up hope of becoming better acquainted with Karen, despite almost always ending up at loggerheads with her whenever they met. His daydream faded as the phone rang out. She could be in the shower, or like him, be out for breakfast, he thought. Clay decided to ring Harold instead.

Harold picked up on the second ring and as if by telepathy guessed it was Clay.

'Good morning, Clay.'

'How do you do that?'

'I listen to my hunches, son. A bit like a soldier on night patrol. If you don't take note of the hair rising on the back of your neck you end up dead. Anyway, have you found a motel room to lie low in?'

'Not exactly a motel room: I'm holed up in that Brighton Beach bathing box you bought for me in,'82.'

'Very creative.' Harold sounded amused.

'What about B.S. Fine Art? Have you any information for me?'

'Yes, I have. It turns out, that Scarlet is no choirboy. I'm not sure you should antagonise him.' Harold's voice was edged with concern. 'If I were you, I'd leave this investigation to the police.'

'I can't, H.G. I find it hard to step away now that I've been framed for Pamela's murder.'

'Scarlet is dangerous, Clay. He has some shady connections with the European underworld. He's suspected of arranging art thefts for notable European underworld clients. No record of having served time, but my contacts in the Met say he's on an Interpol watch list for fraud and money laundering.'

'Looks like he may have opened a branch operation in Melbourne,' Clay quipped.

Not wanting to tell Harold about his plan to bait Scarlet with a fake McCubbin, Clay added, 'Don't worry Harold, I'll pass your information on to the police through Julia and do my best to keep my head down.'

'You could have kept your head down up here in Sydney, Clay.' Harold sounded peeved. Clay didn't try to further defend his need to be in Melbourne, closer to the action. He looked at the remaining coins in his hand; he needed enough to ring Julia, so he asked Harold to mail his findings care of the Brighton Hotel and finished the call by telling Harold he had to make another call.

Harold's revelations only strengthened Clay's suspicion that Scarlet could be involved in Pamela's murder. In his mind, the plan to entrap him became more urgent.

Clay redialled Karen, but all his attempts were fruitless; the phone rang out three more times over the space of an hour. A little exasperated, he rang Julia.

'Blakely Gallery, Julia speaking,' came the efficient response after the first ring.

'I've wasted an hour this morning trying to ring Karen to arrange a visit. For some reason she won't pick up,'

'Oh! Hi Clay. Good morning to you too.'

Clay winced. He'd started off on the wrong foot with Julia again.

'Good morning, Julia,' he said trying a fresh start. 'You see, I'm trying to keep sweet with Karen, I don't want her grumbling about me to the police again.'

'Karen's right, you're only interested in clearing yourself.'

Clay chose not to respond. Instead, he changed the subject. 'Have you spoken with Karen since our meeting?'

'Only once, on Saturday morning, the day after our meeting; she wondered if we were still proceeding with the forged painting plan. She gave me her phone number and address and wanted me to keep her up to date in case you didn't.'

'Oh, I see, you're both chummy enough to swap addresses along with opinions on me,' Clay said, barely disguising his need to score a point.

This time, Julia chose not to respond resulting in an awkward silence. Clay continued, 'I thought I'd take a break from painting our special picture for a few hours and visit Karen. I thought I could check out Pam's room, and possibly find a stronger link to B.S. Fine Art. Julia gave Clay Karen's address on the curt proviso that he ring Karen before turning up, and promptly hung up.

Clay tried two more times to ring Karen without success. Upset and irritated by his niggly conversation

with Julia, Clay returned to the bathing box and sur-
rendered to the act of painting. This delightful distraction enabled Clay to finish the painting around noon.
The loose McCubbin style and alla prima impressionist
technique had enabled Clay to complete the painting
much sooner than he'd originally suggested to Julia
and Karen.

After lunch at the Brighton Beach Hotel, and another unsuccessful call to Karen, Clay decided to head
straight out to the address Julia had given him that
morning.

Chapter Thirteen

Clay walked to Karen's Wrexham Road flat from Windsor Station in a little over ten minutes. Set amongst brick Victorian dwellings with decorative two-tone brickwork and heaps of wrought iron, he found a quiet red brick four-storey group of flats, with cream ground-floor garage doors facing the street.

Karen's unit was on the first floor at the rear. Clay found the ground-floor entrance halfway down the side driveway and climbed the concrete stairs to the first-floor central corridor. Grey-painted doors to each of six units, three on each side lined a dreary passage. Unit six at the south end was Karen's. Clay saw no one about and he figured the building was quiet because most residents were at work.

Clay pressed the white button beside the door to Karen's flat and heard muffled chimes ringing inside. There was no other sound and no one answered the door. Clay tried the button a few more times for the same response. Coming here was a complete waste of time Clay thought, frowning with frustration. In a final capricious gesture, he stepped forward and placed an eye to the security peephole in the vain hope that he might be able to see inside. He couldn't, but while leaning with both hands pressed against the door, he heard a soft click and the door suddenly swung open. The door must have been left unlatched.

Clay stepped back surprised. He looked left and right. The corridor was still empty, unlike Clay's brain, which was beset with possibilities. With only a second's hesitation, Clay pushed the door fully open and stepped into Karen's flat. He gently pulled the door closed behind him, taking care not to lock himself in by not engaging the latch.

Clay stood in a small, tiled entry. To his right, a cloak closet door with an oblong dress mirror attached startled him with an image of his own edgy face and posture. To the left stretched a hall, one wall decorated with framed headshots of Karen and Pamela, the opposite wall contained two closed doors. The hall ended at another door.

'Hello. Hello, Karen, are you there?' Clay called, in a low-pitched voice.

Silence.

Clay called again a little more loudly. 'Hey, Karen, it's Clay.' He paused, cupping his ear to listen. Clay could hear nothing except the sound of a clock ticking somewhere beyond the hall. Karen must be out on a job he thought. Clay was on the wrong side of Karen's door, and his heart started to register his intrusion with a few extra beats per minute. Technically trespassing, but it wasn't as if he was a stranger, well almost but not quite. Technically I haven't broken in he reassured himself, so why not have a quick look through Pam's room? In and out, no harm done.

To his right, two close-set adjacent doors suggested a closet, while opposite the framed headshots the other two doors in the hall looked like entries to bedrooms. One of these doors should open into Pamela's room. Clay grabbed the handle of the nearest door. In and out, that was his intent, but a wave of unease chilled him, and his hand froze. Maybe I should check the living room first before I invade the privacy of their bedrooms, he thought.

Clay tiptoed down the hall to the door he assumed led into the living area. The door was slightly ajar but wouldn't open any further when he pushed on it. Something was jamming it. Clay pushed hard against the door. Gradually the door opened to the sound of scraping, enough to reveal the base of a large, over-turned lamp. Clay reached in, shoved the heavy lamp base out of the way and pushed the door fully open to reveal the living room in total disarray.

The state of the room suggested a desperate struggle. The troublesome lamp had been flung across the room, its power cord at full stretch. Further in, a white leather couch lay upended, its colourful cushions scattered among the remains of a shattered glass-topped coffee table. But what captured Clay's horrified attention most, was the blood trail weaving its way through the chaos to a bloodstained hand towel clumped on the Laminex kitchen bench top.

After a few deep breaths and a futile attempt to dampen an involuntary shiver, Clay took a few tentative steps into the room. Each step revealed further evidence of the intensity of the struggle. Torn curtains hung in front of French doors, which led onto a small south-facing balcony. The television was knocked askew, records, family photos and precious keepsakes were swept from three display shelves on the wall beside the TV. Someone had obviously fallen through the glass coffee table and cut themselves badly enough to bleed freely. Begging the question, was this Karen's blood sprayed across the carpet?

Clay froze mid-step, the cascade of destruction suddenly coalescing into the appalling thought that he might have already walked past Karen's lifeless body in one of the front bedrooms. Clay turned on his heel and looked back toward the hall with trepidation. No wonder Karen hadn't answered his calls. Clay backed up a step, nagged by the need to dispel such a horrible thought, by checking the bedrooms. Clay also realised he didn't want to leave any evidence of his visit which might implicate him in a second murder.

To Clay's horror, the doorbell chimed.

Clay recognised the sound, now much louder inside the flat. At first, he stupidly thought it might be Karen. But no, it couldn't be her, because she would simply use her key and walk straight in. Had to be someone else? Julia maybe? No, no, that's not possible. What reason would Julia have to visit?

'Hello there, hello Karen, it's Senior Constable Parker here.'

Clay's sweat ran cold.

'The bell might be stuffed, give the door a good rap Parker.'

At the sound of Walsh's voice, Clay almost left a urine sample for the detective. Clay's head swivelled like a fairground puppet his mouth open, looking for a place to hide. There was no place, but the balcony offered a slim hope. If the French doors were locked, he was stuffed.

Clay pirouetted and danced between the blood spots and broken glass to the French doors. The cold brass handle resisted just long enough to give Clay's heart a second shock, then yielded. He slipped out onto the balcony, gently closed the doors and slid away from them, his back to the wall. Twenty breathless seconds later Parker and Walsh stumbled over the upturned lamp.

'Whoa! Control yourself, Parker,' Detective Walsh quipped, when Parker spread-eagled on top of Walsh and the lampstand. Parker grunted and climbed to her feet. Parker's expression suggested she'd stepped in dog poo. She quickly moved into the room straightening her uniform as she went.

'Holy shit!' Walsh stood and surveyed the room. 'No need for that warrant you were moaning about outside Parker. If I'm not mistaken that's blood on the floor near the remains of the coffee table, and if so then this mess could easily constitute just cause.'

'Does look suspicious,' Senior Constable Parker replied, now standing at the servery prodding the blood-stained towel with her biro. 'We'll still need to check out the whole flat before jumping to conclusions, but it does look bad for Miss Bunting.'

Keeping his breathing constrained, Clay pressed himself hard against the outside brickwork: he was all ears.

'No wonder you couldn't contact Moray,' Detective Walsh said surveying the room. 'Ten to one she's been done away with, just like that model friend of hers, by that silver-spooned Weston playing the bohemian artist.'

Constable Parker stared at Detective Walsh in disbelief. Obviously wanting to challenge his presumptive opinion.

Clay's shaking intensified at the mention of his name. He suddenly felt trapped and exposed on the small balcony. He eyeballed the drop to the driveway below. Keeping away from the glass doors, he climbed over the balustrade, grabbed the balusters and lowered himself until he hung below the balcony. Clay estimated at least two metres remained to fall. Clay's desire to escape as well as the pain inflicted by the balcony edge tiles cutting into his wrists, made the decision to jump for him. The drop was painless, the landing not so. His knee slammed up into his chin pushing two teeth into his bottom lip. He yelped just a little too loudly.

Walsh threw open the French doors and stepped out onto the balcony.

'Thought I heard something,' he said offhandedly, leaning over the balustrade to peer up and down the driveway leading to Wrexham Road.

Spreadeagled against the wall directly under the balcony Clay held his breath, his hand clamped over his bloody lip.

'Whoever did this is long gone sir,' Constable Parker said, poking her head out between the French doors. 'The blood is dry. We need to check the rest of the flat, find out what neighbours and friends know about Miss Bunting's movements, and if we think she's the subject of foul play, declare this flat a crime scene and call in forensics.'

'Wow Parker! You'll have my job before we get back to the station. And if forensics find that phoney artist's prints all over this flat, we will have him stitched up,' Walsh said, stepping back inside the flat. Constable Parker shook her head, sighed and eyeballed the ceiling.

Clay toe sprinted down the driveway to Wrexham Road. He stalled momentarily at the sight of the police car parked at the curb, but it didn't impede his escape. It was clear to Clay that Karen was in trouble, either abducted or at worst murdered, and that he was in even deeper trouble, because he also realised that he'd left his prints in the flat. The frame was relentlessly tightening like a noose around his neck.

Chapter Fourteen

Clay hated the futility of his visit to Karen's place. He'd failed to find any further links to B.S. Fine Art and had almost been nabbed by Detective Walsh. The only dubious compensation was that he now knew that Karen was in trouble and that Walsh would be after him with renewed vigour. That thought hung over him like a dark glaze.

On his way back to Windsor Station trying not to look like a fugitive, Clay felt very alone and isolated and now wondered if he should have followed H.G.'s advice and stayed in Sydney.

At the station, Clay changed his mind about returning to his Brighton hideout. Instead, he switched platforms and boarded a city-bound train to Richmond Station. Clay wasn't sure how it would help, but he felt the need to confer with Julia.

Richmond Station felt too close to his studio in Cotton Lane. Seeing an occasional patrolling police car made Clay jittery. He'd intended to walk down to Swan

Street and tram-it up Church Street to Blakely Gallery in Waltham Place. But when Clay spotted a second police car cruising up Church Street towards Waltham Place while waiting for a tram, he began to have second thoughts. The fear of blundering into Julia's gallery only to find the police there, prompted him to ring Julia.

Clay slunk into the foyer of the nearby Swan Hotel to find a public phone. He furtively paced the foyer waiting for a free booth.

The phone rang on long enough for Clay to wonder if Julia was out or engaged with a client. He was about to hang up when Julia answered.

'Blakely Gallery, Julia speaking.'

'Julia, thank God you're there. It's Clay,' he said, pausing for breath. 'How are you?' he added, with the memory of their last conversation in mind.

'Oh. Hi Clay. How'd it go with Karen this morning?'

'Not good. Not good at all,' Clay said, struggling for the right words. 'I need to see you.'

'Why? What's wrong?'

'I don't really want to say over the phone,' Clay whispered, glancing over his shoulder at an impatient-looking young man waiting to use the same booth.

'Are you on your own? Is it safe for me to visit the gallery?'

'Yes, to both questions.'

'Have you been visited by them?'

'Them? Oh! You mean the police. Well, yes, I have.' Julia paused, waiting for Clay's response. All Clay did was groan, so Julia continued. 'They came in on Monday. Wanted some background on you. Asked me if I knew Karen's address.'

'Makes sense,' Clay said, talking more to himself than to Julia.

'What makes sense?'

'I'll tell you when I see you. It's too risky for me to visit the gallery with the police sniffing around. Do you think we could meet at the Tre Polli in about half an hour?'

'That little Italian cafe in Chapel Street you used to take me to?'

'Yeah, that's the place.'

'Ok, I suppose I could close the gallery for an hour.' Julia paused to check her diary, during which Clay hung up.

Julia continued talking unaware Clay was no longer on the line. 'I don't have any appointments scheduled for today.'

'Clay? Clay? Are you there?'

'Clay!' Julia flung the phone back onto its cradle.

* * *

Clay was chatting with Giovanni when Julia walked into the Tre Polli. She strode towards Clay looking determined for an altercation but hesitated when Clay turned to reveal a pale taut face.

Giovanni acknowledged Julia with a nod.

'Your usual?'

'A flat white, please,' Julia said, edgily standing beside Clay.

'I remember, even though I've served a few of Clay's — how you say — Belle ragazze...' Giovanni's remark faded in time with the look of rising anguish on Clay's face.

Julia sighed and headed for a table by the window, Clay followed.

They both sat and stared out into Chapel Street in silence till Giovanni brought their coffees.

Their hands touched when they both reached for the sugar.

'You look terrible. What happened to your lip?'

Clay pulled his trembling hand back.

'Julia, I don't know what to do. I'm afraid the same thing that happened to Pamela has happened to Karen.'

'What! Why would you say that? Julia warmed her suddenly cold hands around her coffee cup.

'You haven't seen what I've just seen at Karen's flat,' Clay gasped. The blood, the wrecked room, just like my studio.' Clay cringed over his coffee. 'I don't understand. Why the hell would Scarlet attack Karen? She didn't know anything.'

'You don't know that.'

Clay gave Julia a look of bewilderment. Julia turned to stare out into Chapel Street avoiding Clay's look of reproach. After a lengthy pause, Julia quietly said, 'Maybe she got caught.'

'Caught?'

'Karen told me she needed to— do something.'

'Do something, do what?' Clay said sounding flustered.

'Karen mentioned a stake out, even talked about how she might try to get into B.S. Fine Art after hours.'

'Karen told you all this.'

'Yes. I didn't mention it to you when you rang for her address.' Julia turned back to face Clay. 'Karen was angry. Frustrated with you and your forgery idea, but I didn't think she was serious.'

'My God Julia!' Clay jerked upright in his seat, his face flushing. 'This explains everything. I'll bet Karen went back to spy on B.S. Fine Art and was caught by either Mullet or Scarlet. They both know she's Pamela's concerned friend. If Karen was caught and behaved the way she did the last time we visited, she would have given them heaps of grief. Probably threatened them with the police again.' Breathless, Clay wilted back into his chair.

Julia stared at Clay, aghast.

'If what you say is correct Clay and Karen is still alive, then we must go to the police. What else can we do?'

'Noooo, No way, Julia. I can't.' Clay cast a furtive look left and right. 'That crazy detective Walsh already has me convicted and incarcerated. When I was hiding on Karen's balcony, I overheard his lopsided opinion of me.' Agitated, Clay lurched up to half-standing, almost upsetting the cafe table. 'For Christ's sake, Julia, if what you say is true, we have to do something fast.'

Julia looked up at Clay, startled.

Giovanni also jumped at Clay's sudden outburst.

'You want another cuppa, Clay?'

Julia waved Clay back down with her eyes.

'Yes. Thanks, Giovanni, we'll have the same again, but this time with two serves of Rosa's tasty panettone,' Julia said, pointing to the cafe menu and casting Giovanni a nervous smile. Giovanni's inquisitive look immediately evaporated into one of bounteous enthusiasm. Clay sank back down into his seat and leant across the table.

'Surely, we can fix this ourselves, rather than go to the police,' Clay pleaded, with sudden vigour. 'I'll go back to the bathing box and grab the McCubbin while you contact B.S Fine Art to arrange a valuation.'

Julia shook her head in disbelief.

'Clay, are you serious? Are you sure the fake painting will be enough? Baiting them out with a fake painting in a few days' time is not doing something fast. How's that going to help Karen?'

Giovanni arrived with their panettone and coffee.

'You two are, what you say, thick like thieves,' Giovanni said, giving Clay a wink.

'I think you might have your aphorisms a bit mixed,' Clay said, giving Giovanni an incredulous look. Julia chuckled.

'Me thinks you know what I mean,' Giovanni said, tapping the side of his nose before retreating. Some tension released, they both watched Giovanni cross the floor and disappear into the kitchen to chat with Rosa, before leaning in closer to continue their conversation in quieter tones.

'Karen must have spooked Scarlet big time for him to go after her.' Julia nodded and Clay continued. 'Surely if Karen was a nuisance, they'd only want to shut her up. The blood and evidence of a struggle in her flat suggest they botched the job.' Julia took a few nervous sips of coffee.

'I didn't get a chance to check the bedrooms. I had to take off before those two police checked the rooms, so I don't know if Karen is dead.' Clay flinched at the finality of what he was saying. He took a bite of panettone to suppress a rising lump in his throat. 'Or at best only missing.'

'Being only missing doesn't help poor Pamela,' Julia said, grimly eyeing Clay.

'That's true,' Clay said, fretting panettone crumbs into a small pile. 'We can only hope.' Clay looked Julia straight in the eyes. 'Hope against hope that she's still alive, and if she is, then we need to put some pressure on Scarlet. He needs to know we know he's involved.'

'How the hell are we supposed to do that without resorting to the police?' Julia repeated, a desperate sounding pitch to her question.

Clay avoided Julia's question by facing away and staring silently into Chapel Street. After a moment's thought, Clay took a deep breath and turned back, his face set with grim resolve.

'All right, Clay said. 'There's only one way to do this. I'll go straight down to Oxford Street and confront Scarlet. I'll try and confirm our suspicions and make sure he knows we're on to him.' Julia looked shocked and frightened. Clay reached over and placed his hand on hers.

'It's OK Julia. If I think I'm out of my depth, I promise I'll pull out and go straight to the police.' Clay gave Julia his most reassuring smile. 'As long as you come with me to the police,' he added, with a dopey grin.

'Of course, I'll go with you,' Julia said, patting the back of his hand with her free hand. Clay smiled broadly, and then Julia added, 'After all, I have to protect my investment.' Somewhat deflated, Clay changed the subject.

'Here's my plan. When I go to B.S. Fine Art, I want you to ring Scarlet and arrange a valuation for the fake McCubbin. If you can keep him talking, your call might give me an opportunity to look around while he's distracted.'

'All jokes aside, this sounds like another of your nutty schemes. You're crazy to confront Scarlet, and doubly crazy to try and case the place while he's on the phone. What about Mullet? Your plan doesn't account for him.'

'As I said, Julia, I think talking to the police is a waste of time. But, if you're worried, and you don't hear from me by tomorrow morning, then contact the police anyway, and tell them everything you know.' Julia could see Clay had made his mind up, but feeling the need to keep questioning his crazy plan, she asked, 'Are you sure the painting will look convincing? Won't the paint still be soft?'

Clay's smirk in response to her question, made Julia wonder why she'd bothered to ask.

'The painting is totally convincing. I felt like I was channelling McCubbin while painting on the very same beach McCubbin frequented in the 1890s.' Besotted by the memory, Clay expounded on the brilliance of his painting technique. 'It's a damn sight more convincing than those Streeton fakes Scarlet's been pedalling. Hell, I even managed to imitate the craquelure by heating a final epoxy glaze with a gas torch. The paint surface looks old and as hard as your investment strategy.'

Julia bared her teeth at him.

'Gotcha,' Clay said, and smiled.

'Lame joke, Clay,' Julia said, standing.

'I must get back to the gallery. Give me about half an hour, then I'll ring Scarlet and try to keep him talking, before I close for the day.'

Julia headed for the door and cast Clay a final worried look before leaving. Clay watched Julia walk up Chapel Street and hail a taxi.

Chapter Fifteen

Cradling another coffee in the Tre Polli, Clay reconsidered what Julia had said about calling the police. Clay had time to kill while Julia returned to Blakely Gallery. Why not use the time to ring the police? The whole murder fiasco he was entangled in was becoming tiresome. Maybe Julia had a point; maybe he was paranoid thinking the police had it in for him. Why not let the police untangle the mess?

Clay could safely use Giovanni's public phone to call the police. Surely calling to tell them why he suspected Scarlet was an indication of his innocence. If he'd murdered Pamela or Karen, wouldn't he be keeping as far from the police as possible? It all seemed logical to Clay.

Clay swallowed the last of his coffee, grabbed some coins from Giovanni, found the number for Richmond Police Station in the phone book, and dialled. Officer Jon Bruce in reception answered, and Clay asked to speak with the detectives investigating the Pamela

Moray murder. Officer Bruce asked the nature of his call and his name. Clay chose to remain anonymous but insisted he had useful information.

'Oh yeah. We get useful information all the time.' The duty placed Clay on hold. Clay waited for what seemed like ages, while his mind toyed with the notion that Officer Bruce was busy tracing his call. But that sort of thing only happens in Charlie's Angels.

'Senior Constable Parker speaking. Do you believe you have some information pertinent to the Pamela Moray murder?'

'Ah, Parker. You're the officer that visited my studio with Detective Walsh, right?'

Parker did not reply immediately. During the pause, Clay heard papers shuffled, the thump and scratch of a dropped phone handpiece and a frenzy of whispered commands.

'Yes, I am. And you're Clay Weston, right?' the slightly breathless Senior Constable Parker asked.

'I guess.'

'Either you are, or you aren't, and if you are, then thank you for ringing Clay.'

'Yes, it's me, I mean... Yes, I am Clay Weston.'

'Ok Clay, that's a good start. Now we know that you're back in Melbourne, why don't you tell me where you are so we can have a proper talk.'

'How do you know I'm in Melbourne, I could be phoning from any —'

'— No STD pips on the connection.'

'Oh! I guess you're right,' Clay said, wincing at his own stupidity.

'I know I'm right. So how about that proper talk?'

'We are having a proper talk,' Clay said, becoming a little anxious at the direction the conversation was taking.

'I mean face to face,' Parker persisted.

'Come on, I'm not that stupid,' Clay said, his anxiety turning to frustration. 'Look. I didn't have anything to do with poor Pamela's death. I only rang to tell you what I do know.'

'All right Clay. You tell me what you know.'

'Well, I know that the blood in Karen's flat isn't mine.'

'We found your prints and now you brazenly admit to being in Karen Bunting's flat?'

'Yes, I was, but...' Clay gulped, the conversation was definitely not going as he imagined.

'Clay?'

'Yes.'

'What have you done with Karen?'

'What do you mean?'

'She's missing.'

'Nothing, damn it! I haven't done anything with her. I have no idea where she is. Can't you see I'm only trying to help you find the real per —'

'— Clay, the best way you could help, would be to come in so we can question you.' Parker paused for Clay's reply, he didn't respond, so she continued, 'And then you let the police do the investigating.'

'I'm, I'm not so sure about that Constable Parker. I've been framed and Detective Walsh can't see it.' Constable Parker said nothing, and the silence felt ominous to Clay. Clay's paranoia rose. Could Parker be trying to trace his call? Clay was about to hang up when Constable Parker broke back in.

'Framed, you say. Why would you think that?'

'Well for starters. That night when you and Detective Walsh helped me break into my studio, Pamela wasn't there. Her clothes were still on my couch, and my painting of her, the one her body was wrapped in, the one you commented on, was still on my easel —'

'— But we didn't really search your studio that night. I never saw her clothes and Pamela could have been lying dead up in your loft.'

'If you don't interrupt and let me finish, I'll explain,' Clay said, his voice cracking with anxiety.

'I know, I know. I thought Pam was flaked out on weed up in my loft. So, I didn't encourage you and Detective Walsh to hang around and search. I was trying to get rid of you, so Pam wouldn't get busted for possession.' Clay took a deep breath and continued.

'You see, Pamela wasn't in my studio, she was missing, and it was all a bit of a mystery to me. Then, the next morning when Karen turned up looking for Pam, we found a business card amongst Pam's clothes linking her to B.S. Fine Art in Oxford Street. Karen and I believed that Pamela applied for a gallery hostess position at B.S. Fine Art, so we paid them a visit to see if they knew anything. Barry Scarlet, the proprietor, claimed he'd never seen Pamela, which was strange. Then, straight after that visit to B.S Fine Art, my studio is broken into, trashed, and that painting of Pamela and her clothes vanishes. You saw my trashed studio on your second visit. A visit prompted by Karen's complaint, that I was the last person to see Pamela. What you didn't notice that second time, was that Pam's clothes and the painting were gone. When they turned up in the dumpster with Pam's body... voila! I'm suddenly the prime suspect.' Clay paused to let his explanation sink in.

Constable Parker didn't wait long. 'Yeah, but you ran when we told you to stay in Melbourne.'

'I didn't run,' Clay quickly responded. 'I went to a meeting in Sydney. I had no idea I was being set up. I underestimated the trouble that Pamela's murderer would go to, to cover his tracks. Bear with me Parker, because it gets better. When I returned to Melbourne, I discovered from Julia Blakely, who as you know is my gallery dealer, that Karen had told her she wanted to visit B.S Fine Art to question Scarlet again. And guess what happened next?'

'I can't guess Clay, but I'm sure you're going to tell me.' Constable Parker sounded irritated.

'You're dead right, I am going to tell you,' Clay said, labouring the point. 'What happened next Constable Parker, was that Karen went missing just like Pamela. I visited her flat looking for her, and found it wrecked and splatted in blood and bingo! I'm in the frame for a second murder.'

'Yes Clay, you're right; you are a suspect in Karen's disappearance and possible murder. I hope you realise, that I'm recording this call. By not coming in for questioning you may be digging an even deeper hole for yourself. You sure have it in for this Scarlet character. All on the flimsiest of circumstantial evidence I've ever heard.' Parker paused: during which, Clay could hear voices in the background. Clay suspected Parker was trying to initiate a phone tap with her office colleagues. He took the opportunity provided by Parker's pause to jump back into his defence.

'You say the evidence is flimsy, but I've only given you a brief outline of my dealings with B.S Fine Art. I've had my business manager in Sydney check out Scarlet's connections, and it turns out he's under suspicion in Europe for art fraud, so from my perspective, the evidence isn't that flimsy.'

'All I can say, Clay, is that if you come into Richmond Station, and tell us everything you know,' Parker said, trying to sound conciliatory, 'I'll do my best to follow up on any leads you might suggest.'

'I don't think I can do that just yet. I'm only ringing because Julia advised me to. I've followed her advice and I'm still not convinced it's in my best interest to speak with you in person.'

'Don't hang up,' Constable Parker quickly said, hearing the despair in Clay's voice.

'Why? What's the point?'

'Time, I need time,' Parker said.

'Time for what?'

'Umm, you know. Time to investigate this Barry Scar —'

'— Yeah, time to trace this call, that's what you need.' Clay said, more to himself than to Parker, as he gently replaced the receiver.

Clay looked across the Tre Polli and saw Giovanni, slowly drying cutlery while watching him from behind the counter. Clay gave Giovanni a nonchalant wave of thanks and headed for the door. Julia would be back at Blakely Gallery and trying to ring Scarlet. It was time to visit B.S. Fine Art again.

Chapter Sixteen

'Weston's back in Melbourne.' Detective Walsh looked up from his paperwork at the sound of Senior Constable Parker's announcement.

'How do you know?' Walsh queried, gathering up papers in front of him. 'Damn paperwork is smothering effective police work.' He dumped the sheaf of papers in the out tray of his desk.

Constable Parker stepped into Walsh's office, closed the door behind her and approached his desk.

'Just had a phone convo with him. He tried to drop some information on us anonymously, but he's pretty naive when it comes to cloak-and-dagger stuff.'

'Ha ha. Naive? Not likely. Look at the front he's established for himself.'

'Front?' Parker said, trying to cover her expression of surprise by turning to pull up a worn office chair in front of Walsh's desk.

'Well, he's a millionaire rich kid; a company director mind you. Playing at being the bohemian artist, with no phone and no car. The whole deal's a front for a nice little porn lair in Richmond.'

'Surely you don't think Weston's got the Blakely Gallery conned as well, because I checked out Julia Blakely, his art dealer, and according to the boffins at the National Gallery she's legit.'

'All part of a good con job, Parker, that's gone a bit pear-shaped for him now. What I can't figure is how he gave us the slip. Our fault I suppose, we telegraphed our intentions by questioning him just before we found Moray's body.'

Walsh eyed Parker in expectation of agreement. Parker squirmed in her chair.

'Well, Parker, what did the prick tell you? Anything useful we can use to find him?'

Constable Parker related the gist of her conversation with Clay.

'Shit! Reckons he's been framed now, does he? Sounds like the sort of story a good defence lawyer might cook up.'

'Even so, I thought we should check out B.S. Fine Art and have a chat with this Barry Scarlet.'

Detective Walsh ignored Parker's suggestion, grabbed another pile of forms from his inbox, and bent to shuffle through them before replying.

'Fine. You have a chat with Scarlet. The minute I clear my fricking desk, I'm going to boost the search intensity on Weston, especially now I know he's back in Melbourne.'

Parker nodded, stood up and left Walsh's office with a pained expression.

Chapter Seventeen

Clay wasn't sure how long he'd spent wasting his time talking to Senior Constable Parker, but he figured he didn't have much of the half-hour Julia had allocated to return to Blakely Gallery and phone B.S. Fine Art. Clay left the Tre Polli and headed down to Oxford Street at a fast walk.

Clay slowed his pace, the moment he turned into Oxford Street. The street was no longer the quiet side street he and Karen had encountered on their first visit. Now, a crowd of about twenty-five people were gathered at the entrance to B.S. Fine Art. Clay walked up and mingled. Taped to the closed door of the gallery, a small poster advertised a 5 PM exhibition viewing for art investors.

Clay's spacey ZZ Top T-shirt, black jeans and blue and white pin stripped sneakers contrasted with the conservative business suits worn by the waiting group of wealthy Toorak and South Yarra art investors. Fortunately, he recognised a couple of faces in the crowd.

People he'd seen at his one-man exhibitions at Blakely Gallery. One, whose name escaped him, smiled and nodded in recognition. Clay nodded back, now feeling more confident his inappropriate attire would be excused by at least some of the crowd. In fact, he could see that word of his appearance was being passed around.

How convenient, Clay thought. This little soiree will let me get in this time without having to bullshit my way past Mullet. However, he knew his attire would stand out the way a small splash of complementary colour engaged the eye in a painting. Barry Scarlet or Terry Mullet would probably spot him the moment he entered, but they would also be reluctant to create a scene. Though, he felt sure Scarlet would want to engage with him, if only to persuade him to leave.

Right on 5 PM the door to the gallery opened and the small crowd politely jostled into the expensive glow of the halogen exhibition lighting. Clay allowed about two thirds of the cluster to enter before he breached the entrance. He noticed that the green grey walls were still covered with the same individually lit paintings as those he'd seen with Karen almost a week prior. Tonight however, the overhead lighting was lit for the crowd, which brightened the space and dispelled the darker ambience of his previous visit. Clay wondered if any of the chirpy prospective investors had misgivings about the veracity of the art surrounding them.

Neither Scarlet nor Mullet was present. A young woman, no doubt the new exhibition hostess, had opened the door. She was dressed in a black and white striped pastiche of a 19th Century dinner dress. She gave the impression she'd stepped straight from one of Streeton's paintings. This little promotional trick was accompanied by a titter of oohs and ahhs as the girl effusively welcomed each person into the gallery.

Clay spotted the open office door at the far end of the gallery from which Scarlet had entered on Clay's previous visit. The hostess having finished greeting most of the customers glided through this doorway and almost immediately returned with a silver tray of finger food. Terry Mullet appeared behind the hostess with a tray of champagne flutes; they both began to circulate around the gallery. To avoid Mullet, Clay chose to circulate in the opposite direction. Clay had no doubt that Mullet would soon spot him despite his efforts to keep clutches of people between them. Was Scarlet still in the office? Clay would soon know, he had almost reached the point where he could look in through the open doorway, when one of the faces he recognised outside in Oxford Street, tapped him on the shoulder.

'You're Clay Weston the artist, aren't you?'

Clay turned to face a portly, mid-fifties man, wearing a white suit, blue pinstripe shirt and large blue bow tie.

'Ah, yes, you've tagged me.' Clay searched his memory for the man's name. According to Julia, Clay never paid enough attention to the tastemakers. Clay preferred to leave this aspect of his art practice to Julia. Now he found himself confronted by the need to remember this man's name, whom he thought might be either an art critic or a prominent Melbourne art investor.

'Well, Mr. Weston, have you an opinion on the authenticity of some of these works?' the man asked, waving his hand to encompass the paintings on the nearest wall.

Clay was surprised that someone other than him suspected the probity of the paintings.

'Do you write about art for one of the dailies?' Clay enquired, fishing for some scrap of information that might help identify the man.

'Sometimes my research ends up in the odd rag,' the man said, unable to disguise his intellectual disdain for the tabloid press.

Clay smiled at this display of snobbery but nodded.

'Which institution is it that you work for?' Clay asked, still fishing, at the same time peering over the man's shoulder to locate Mullet, who had now circulated further around the room and was almost upon them. Clay needed to remove himself from the conversation in order to move away from Mullet if he was to get a look in through the office door.

'Please excuse me.' Clay started to edge away. 'I'm sure my opinion as an artist is irrelevant, but you may be onto something regarding the credibility of this exhibition.' Won't hurt to get the word out about Scarlet's fakes, Clay thought.

Clay wondered if he would be able to remain unnoticed before Julia's telephone call diversion. A brief look through the crowd to locate Mullet, found him no longer circulating. Mullet now stood dead still, a laser stare focused on Clay. Clay kept moving toward the office door. In that instant of recognition, Mullet, who was almost on the other side of the gallery, began moving to intercept Clay. On the way, he deposited the champagne tray on a narrow hall table against one wall.

Clay was taking a quick peek inside the office just as Mullet caught hold of his elbow. Clay turned to confront Mullet. He'd seen Scarlet sitting behind a large oak desk speaking on the phone.

Clay looked down at Mullet with disdain, easily shaking Mullet's grip from his elbow. Despite the better lighting, Mullet's greasy appearance had not improved since their last encounter. For the exhibition opening, he'd tried to dress up but failed. His not quite pressed black tux failed to suggest any semblance of refinement, his frilly grey and white dress shirt punctuated by a puce pink bow tie buttoned over his smoker's chest, reminded Clay of Smarty the weasel character from Disney's Toon Patrol. Though what attracted

Clay's attention most was Mullet's bandaged left hand, which the drinks' tray had previously obscured.

Mullet's bandaged hand nourished a small seed of hope in Clay's mind. Maybe, just maybe, the blood at Karen's place might not have been hers. This faint hope suggested that Karen might still be alive.

Mullet noticed Clay staring at his hand, which he diffidently placed out of sight in his jacket pocket.

'What the hell are you doin' here anyway? I thought you got the message last time,' Mullet grunted, shoving up against Clay to intimidate and possibly move Clay toward the exit. Clay stood his ground, he easily outweighed Mullet.

'Not very friendly of you,' Clay said, pushing Mullet back with one hand. Mullet's untidy brows lowered over an ugly glare. 'What happened to your hand? Have an accident with a glass coffee table, did you?' Clay watched for Mullet's reaction.

'None of your f'in business,' Mullet said, a little too loudly. Suddenly aware of heads turning in the crowd, to whom he gave an exasperated glare, he added under his breath, 'It's nothing to the accident you might 'ave.' He turned his attention back to the concerned art patrons and covered his anger for their benefit with an exaggerated smile. They shuffled away to a discrete distance; no doubt repelled by Mullet's yellow-toothed grin.

Mullet turned back to Clay, the veins in his neck rising. 'I've never been near that bitch Karen or her flat in Prahran.'

Clay fixed Mullet with a triumphant look. 'I never mentioned Karen's name or her flat,' he said, rubbing in his remark at Mullet's dopey admission with a cheeky smile.

Mullet's face took on the air of an approaching storm. He pulled his bandaged hand from his pocket, now fisted around a closed flick knife. Clay glanced left and right looking for an escape route, then adopted a defensive posture waiting for Mullet's next move. As if by magic, Barry Scarlet appeared behind Mullet and placed a big hand on Mullet's left shoulder. Mullet swung around as if under attack, but seeing it was Scarlet, he pocketed the knife and retreated behind his boss.

'I'll deal with Mr. Weston.' He said, turning to face Clay. 'You seem to be in dispute with my manager again, Mr. Weston.'

'Mr Scarlet, I'd like to ask you — '

Scarlet held up both hands to interrupt.

'— As I said last time we met, I don't think B.S. Fine Art can help you with a valuation at this time.'

Clay was amazed at Scarlet's cool cockiness, but he was determined to accomplish the goal of his visit.

'Actually, I came to tell you that I now know that Pamela Moray applied for your gallery hostess position.'

Clay nodded in the direction of the costumed hostess serving the last of the finger food. 'Your claim to have not met her is untrue.'

'Really, Mr. Weston,' Scarlet said, raising a smug eyebrow. 'I can't be expected to remember every girl who applies for a position here.'

'I also know that Karen Bunting, the girl with me on my last visit, returned here to ask about Pamela,' Clay's voice rose. 'And now it appears that she may also have experienced a similar fate to her friend.'

'What are you implying Weston?' Scarlet asked coolly.

Some of the exhibition crowd nervously looked in the direction of the commotion.

Clay waved a finger in Scarlet's face.

'Listen Scarlet — '

—Scarlet moved in close to Clay, pushed Clay's finger aside and lowered his voice to a coarse whisper.

'Allegations from someone this morning's papers describe as, a wanted murderer, are quite frankly a joke.' Scarlet beckoned to Mullet who was standing off to one side with an asinine grin.

'Call the police, Terry. I do believe we've heard enough crap from this murderer, or should I say, serial killer?'

'Yes, boss. You is dead right boss. I'll ring 'em right away.' Mullet looked a little stunned by his boss's sudden reaffirmation, and feeling the need to say something more supportive added, 'It's ridiculous eh, boss, to think we would have his nosey girlfriend bound and gagged in our store...'

Scarlet winced and gave Mullet a brass-knuckled look that gagged him in mid-sentence. Mullet backed towards the office bewildered.

Clay noticed that the mood in the gallery had shifted to that of mild panic. Those nearest the altercation had started to retreat. Scarlet noticed the change too and reacted to the mini exodus by stepping away from Clay and cajoling the crowd to remain. Seeing his efforts were ineffective, he motioned to the hostess to help.

Clay took the opportunity provided by the distraction to slide towards the exit; he didn't want to be the only person left in the gallery with Scarlet, or the police. Clay mingled with the departing patrons and followed the white-suited art critic whose name still escaped him, out into Oxford Street. Any embarrassment Clay might experience from a renewed conversation with an unnamed critic would be preferable to what he would experience with Scarlet or the police.

Chapter Eighteen

A cold wind tugged at Clay's T-shirt as he stepped into Oxford Street and quickly headed for a Chapel Street tram. Clay shivered more with indecision than the cold as he fast-walked to the tram stop. With no tram in sight and despite the threat of rain, Clay changed his mind and decided to walk to South Yarra Station rather than tram it. The walk would give him time to think.

The prearranged distraction at B.S. Fine Art that he'd cooked up with Julia hadn't worked out the way he'd imagined, and his confrontation with Mullet and Scarlet had yielded little on Karen's fate. All that he'd established, mostly through Mullet's stupidity, was that Karen had visited the gallery a second time, and that Mullet may have left the blood trail in Karen's flat. Mullet's quip, cut short by an impatient Scarlet, that Karen or his girlfriend, as Mullet described her, was bound and gagged in B.S Fine Art's storeroom was clearly designed to rile Clay. Scarlet would never have suggested the police be called if Karen was hidden in the building.

It did seem to Clay, that Julia was correct to describe his attempt to pressure Scarlet as another of his crazy plans. The plan's failure had yielded a miserable cache of information, none of which would convince the police to drop their pursuit of him. All Clay had achieved was to reveal that he was back in Melbourne, and Clay felt sure that Scarlet would dob him in to the police as soon as he could.

Depressed by these events, Clay felt the need to commiserate with Julia. He wanted to report what little he'd gleaned, but he knew that Blakely Gallery would now be closed for the day. Julia would have gone home to her well-kept renovated Edwardian house in Type Street, Richmond.

Clay could ring Julia, but he'd not rung her at home since their art school liaison. Their relationship now was one of a purely business nature. Clay felt reluctant to renew that small intimacy. An intimacy Clay missed. Due to the testiness of their recent encounters; he decided to wait until tomorrow. In the meantime, Clay would return to his bathing box hideout and parcel up the McCubbin for delivery to Julia tomorrow. Clay walked with increasing gloom; he was starting to doubt the potential of his plan to entrap Scarlet.

At South Yarra Station Clay boarded a silver Sandringham Line train to Brighton. On board, he sat with his head down and eyes closed mulling over his confrontation with Mullet and Scarlet. Clay figured his visit to B.S. Fine Art had not been a complete disaster. Despite the lack of evidence, Clay was now even more convinced that Mullet was involved with Karen's disappearance.

Pulled from his thoughts by the carriage's shuddering stop at Prahran, the first station down from South Yarra, Clay looked up aimlessly and caught a peripheral glimpse of a familiar rat-like face.

Mullet was lounging in the next carriage, watching Clay through the windows of the connecting carriage doors from behind an unconvincingly spread copy of The Sun.

Clay averted his gaze and pretended to be oblivious by slumping back into a relaxed posture and feigning sleep. Despite Clay's appearance, his mind was at full attention. Clay's first thought — surely Mullet can't read — tweaked his lips into a smile. Clay's next thought focused on the fact that Mullet was following him. If Mullet was following him immediately after his visit to B.S. Fine Art, then Scarlet must be rattled.

Not wanting to lead Mullet to his bathing box refuge, Clay decided to leave the train at the next station, only minutes away. When the train pulled to a halt at Windsor Station, Clay quickly rose and exited. He walked swiftly down the platform to the street exit, pausing at the exit gate just long enough to show the station clerk his rail pass, and for Mullet to see him turn into Maddock Street. With Mullet firmly in tow, but not yet able to see which way he was headed, Clay sprinted across Maddock Street and ducked down a cobble-stoned service lane.

This lane behind the Chapel Street businesses was filled with overflowing dumpsters, stacked wooden pallets, piles of cardboard boxes and the odd delivery van parked along its length.

Long sunset shadows now provided sufficient cover for Clay to hide behind a dumpster. A moment later he spotted Mullet hurry past the entrance to the lane, headed in the direction of Chapel Street. Mullet gave the lane only a cursory glance, no doubt assuming Clay was in Chapel Street.

Mullet had lost his quarry and had no idea that the tables were now turned. In the fading light, Clay easily followed Mullet, who returned by train to meet up with Barry Scarlet outside B.S. Fine Art.

Clay watched them from a vantage point in Chapel Street. He saw Scarlet waving his fist, pointing and gesticulating wildly at a cowering Mullet. It was clear Mullet was getting ticked off for his failure. Moments later Scarlet left, his black Jaguar turning into Chapel Street with an angry squeal of tyres to merge with the evening rush hour traffic.

If Mullet called a taxi or had a car parked close by, Clay would have nothing left but to return to Brighton.

However, Mullet left Oxford Street on foot heading towards South Yarra Station. Clay was surprised but thought he had nothing to lose by continuing the tail. Clay was doubly surprised a short time later when Mullet caught a city-bound train and travelled only one stop to Richmond. Mullet exited onto Swan Street, Clay's familiar home territory. Clay followed taking advantage of his knowledge of every recessed door and laneway. But when Clay took his eyes off his target to avoid oncoming traffic while crossing to the other side of Swan Street, Mullet vanished.

'Shit! Where'd he go?' Clay cursed. Clay scanned left and right.

The only businesses open were restaurants and takeaways. Mullet must have ducked into one, but which one and why? Could he live out back or upstairs in one of these businesses? If he did, then Clay's tail was a dead loss. Clay didn't want to get caught peering in through the windows of each business, so he paced up and down on his side of Swan Street.

After ten minutes, Clay was about to give up when Mullet suddenly appeared almost opposite him in the doorway of The Chicken Bar, with his hands full of large fast food takeaway bags.

He's only collected dinner, something I could do with, Clay thought, turning his back to Mullet to avoid recognition. Mullet carried his purchases towards the station. Clay followed with the sinking feeling that all this cloak and dagger work was simply keeping him from his own dinner; maybe he should confront Mullet and invite himself for dinner. Mullet was carrying a lot of takeaway for a scrawny runt. Clay continued his tail, observing from his side of Swan Street. However, under the Swan Street rail bridge, Mullet suddenly crossed onto the same side as Clay veered left into Cremorne Street and then turned left again into Stephenson Street.

The prow of the triangular A1 Art Imports building jutted into view. Clay had walked past this building a thousand times. One day on impulse, he'd decided to check the place out.

When the manager of A1 Art Imports saw Clay, he assumed Clay was another unemployed art student looking for work, and launched into an introductory spiel about how each artist they employed could earn five dollars per painting. The manager continued with how easy it was to make good money, painting quickly without the need to think. Artists were employed to simply follow a provided template painting. All each artist had to do, was paint the same pictures over and over, until he could paint them in his sleep. Their quality control was stringent. Each painting had to be indistinguishable from the imported Taiwanese sample. Clay didn't stay to listen to the entire pitch; he excused himself with a promise to think about the offer. The fact that A1 Art Imports thrived was indicative of the low level of art appreciation amongst the average Australian punter.

Mullet's on a direct route to my studio Clay thought, dawdling a little to allow Mullet to stay far enough in front. Mullet must live near my studio Clay thought, blithely walking the familiar path on autopilot; Clay almost missed Mullet's turn into Dover Street, one street behind Clay's studio.

Clay hung back at the corner and watched him approach a factory building that must have almost backed onto his studio in Cotton Lane. Mullet looked left and right before slipping down a concrete side path on the south side of the building and disappearing from Clay's view.

Clay waited a few minutes before approaching what seemed to him to be very strange accommodations. On second thought, who was he to think Mullet's choice of digs strange, when he lived in a converted factory just around the corner? A short distance down the side path, a steel mesh fence containing a padlocked steel mesh gate blocked access to the rear of the property. Just beyond the gate Clay could see a side entrance door into the factory.

Clay hung back in the shadows to scan the red brick building, which was an idle auto repair shop, very much like his own ex-engineering shop. A hand-painted FOR SALE sign was wired to the iron grill over a single street-facing frosted window. Between the window and a roller door was a standard on-street entry door. No lights were visible and now that Mullet was inside there was no sound.

Clay remembered the chaos of his trashed studio, which he now suspected was Mullet's work, and wondered if he should bang on the door and harass the weasel in his own place.

Without warning, Clay heard the scrape of the side door opening through which Mullet had entered. Clay would be caught loitering on the footpath directly across the road in front of the place if he didn't quickly find a place to hide. Clay skittered further down Dover Street and backed into the protective shadows of a handy recessed entry.

Clay wondered, surely he hasn't had time to eat the entire chicken takeaway? Mullet unlocked the chain-mesh gate passed through and relocked it before he appeared at the footpath, now carrying only one small bag of takeaway. He cautiously scanned the street before stalking back towards Richmond Station. Clay watched Mullet until he turned out of Dover Street.

Clay began to follow Mullet down Dover Street. Should I continue to follow, he wondered? This surveillance could go on all night. Maybe I'm wasting my time, Clay rationalised over the sound of his rumbling stomach.

'Food, that's what I really need,' Clay muttered, 'and... Yes! That is exactly what Karen would need too!'

Clay silently whooped, slicing the night air with an affirming punch. All Clay had to do was ring the police, and they would search the place and rescue, Karen.

Buoyed by this realisation, Clay broke off his pursuit of Mullet, turned around and returned to the auto shop to see if he could find some physical evidence to support his contention. Clay examined the building as he crept down the side path to the chain mesh gate. The gate was secured with an old padlock, was a good two metres high and capped with a tangle of rusty barbed wire. Beyond the gate further down the path Clay could just see the timber panel side entrance through which Mullet had entered. There were no windows along the entire length of the wall, and no doubt the door would also be locked.

Clay returned to the street and hammered on the front roller door with his fists. He paused periodically to listen but heard nothing. If Karen was being held in here, she must be secured in a room at the rear. If Karen yelled for help would Clay even hear her? With no evidence for his hunch, apart from the food clue and the short time Mullet spent in the building, Clay started to wonder if he could be wrong. Was Karen even there at all?

This last disconcerting thought took the gloss off Clay's previous assumption. The thought that he might be wrong began to temper his desire to race to the police. If Mullet left food for Karen, then, Clay figured, she'd be safe till morning.

He'd come back first thing tomorrow with bolt cutters and a crowbar, break in and confirm his theory.

As Clay walked back towards Richmond Station, he felt uneasy about the possibility of leaving Karen imprisoned for another night, but his belief that he was the person best equipped to find Karen was much stronger than his faith in the police. 'The minute I do find her I'll call the police,' Clay issued a sigh of resignation into Richmond's cool night air.

Chapter Nineteen

Clay did not sleep well, being constantly woken by unsettling dreams of Karen's imprisonment.

At first light, the dump and hiss of a rising surf, lifted by an approaching southerly dragged Clay from his camp bed. The cold slap and sting of the salty Brighton Bay water cleared some of Clay's guilt-induced mental scumble.

Clay wrapped and tied the fake McCubbin in a clean beach towel and tidied up his bathing box, motivated by the hope that if he was successful in rescuing Karen, then he would no longer need to return.

Clay strode into the Beach Hotel with the wrapped McCubbin under his arm at half past seven, for what he hoped would be his last breakfast as a fugitive.

'You're in early today, I've only just opened,' Red said, pulling chairs from atop the tables.

'I have some early business.' Clay didn't elaborate and Red didn't push it. 'I need some change for the phone mate.'

'Righto.' Red moved to the till. 'Cook's been in since seven, are you up for your usual brekkie?'

Clay nodded, dropped ten dollars on the counter, and then waited for Red's change in coins. Clay nodded a thank you and walked across to the public phone.

He would have to ring Julia at home; it was too early for her to be at Blakely Gallery. Karen's predicament made Clay increasingly anxious to return to the disused auto repair shop in Richmond as soon as possible.

'Hi Julia, it's Clay. I'm sorry to ring you at home.'

'Oh. Hi, Clay. No problem. In fact, I was a bit worried when I didn't hear from you last night after you confronted B.S. Fine Art.'

'I didn't want to ring you at home. You know. It's been a while...'

There was a moment of dead air.

'Did my little diversion work?' Julia asked, to bring the pause to an end. 'I did manage to speak with Scarlet and arranged for the McCubbin to be valued on Friday.'

'I think I spotted Scarlet on the phone when I was having a bit of trouble with Mullet. But in truth, it turned out to be another of my lame ideas. Anyway, it ended up being a very profitable night.'

'Why was that?'

Clay quickly related the events of the previous night including his suspicion that Karen might be imprisoned in the vacant auto shop behind his studio.

'Are you going to ring the police, Clay?'

'I have. I rang them after we met last night at the Tre Polli. I don't think they believed a word I said.'

'Did you tell them everything you told me?'

'Pretty much, but I got the impression that I dug myself in deeper. The fact that I'd been to Karen's blood-spattered flat only connected me with another victim. Now they probably think I'm a serial killer.'

'Clay, you need to ring them again and tell them what you discovered after following Mullet.'

'I will Julia, trust me.'

'You don't sound too convincing.'

If Julia had seen Clay wince at her suggestion, she would have done more than doubt his conviction.

'I'll drop the McCubbin into you this morning.'

'Are you sure we need the forgery plan now?'

'I think the McCubbin is even more relevant now.'

'How's that?'

'Because of what I didn't tell you yesterday. You see, I spoke with Harold Garter on Tuesday, and he told me that Scarlet is on an Interpol watch list for money laundering and the distribution of stolen art throughout the European art market.'

'Really? That's big! He sounds dangerous Clay.'

'Yeah, that's what Harold said. Even if the police nab Mullet for Karen's abduction, Scarlet's obviously the brains, and I'm sure he will have covered his own arse. A little extra evidence, like art fraud, might be useful.'

Clay spotted Red waving.

'I gotta go, Julia, my breakfast's ready. I'll catch you later this morning.'

'Ok, I'll look forward to seeing you after I open. Don't forget to contact the police, and please be careful.'

Clay hung up, joined Red at the bar and started downing his fry-up.

'Wife trouble?' Red asked, nodding towards the phone booth.

Clay stopped chewing and looked up.

'Why would you say that?' he asked around a mouthful of fried egg on toast.

'Cause one of the regulars reckons he's seen you shacked up in a bathing box up on Middle Brighton Beach. I thought, maybe the missus might 'ave kicked you out.'

'Jesus! No. I'm not married. Julia's only my agent. My art dealer. I'm not in a relationshi —'

'— Well, I'm not one to pry mate, but you have generated a bit of discussion here in the bar.'

'I've got a few accommodation issues at the present. I should have it all sorted today.'

Red's puzzled look changed into his usual broad smile. 'More coffee, Clay?'

Chapter Twenty

Senior Constable Parker visited B.S. Fine Art early on Wednesday morning after the Art Investors Exhibition that Clay had attended. S.C. Parker was unaware of the lazy business hours held by art galleries. B.S. Fine Art normally did not open until 10 AM, but Parker bumped into Ajax Cleaners exiting via the Oxford Street entrance when she arrived.

Barry Scarlet was about to lock up after the cleaners when S.C. Parker confronted him.

'Excuse me,' Parker said, approaching Scarlet. I'm Senior Constable Parker from Richmond Station. I'd like to ask you a few questions pertaining to the murder of Pamela Moray.

Scarlet smiled and invited Parker into the gallery. Parker noted his slight Italian accent, expensive European suit, patent leather shoes, super fine shirt and silk tie, which reminded her of the clobber worn by criminal drug importers. Scarlet pocketed his gold-rimmed sunglasses, which capped off his Mafia look for Parker as she started with the questions.

'Can you confirm that Miss Moray applied for a hostess position here?

'She may have. I can't remember the names of all the girls who applied, and Terry my gallery manager, interviewed others that I didn't see for the position.'

Scarlet did not exhibit any body language that would indicate he was uncomfortable with Parker's line of questioning. If anything, he exuded supreme confidence. S.C. Parker persisted.

'Do you remember her girlfriend Karen Bunting, visiting and asking about Miss Moray?'

Scarlet stroked his chin, his head tilted towards the ceiling as if tracking a distant memory. 'I do have a vague recollection; however, my memory includes her being accompanied by a belligerent fellow who had an altercation with my gallery manager.'

'Can you remember the name of that belligerent fellow?'

'I think his name was Weston,' Scarlet said, a degree of uncertainty in his voice. 'Yes, I think it was Clay Weston. I believe I recognised him from exhibition catalogues and newspaper articles. He's a minor painter with an inflated public profile. Some of these younger artists are irresponsible bounders with no respect for traditional painting or values.'

'Do you know what the confrontation was about?' SC Parker asked, moving on with her line of questioning.

'Weston claimed he wanted a valuation for paintings Miss Bunting had acquired as part of a deceased estate. I believe he was taking advantage of Miss Bunting. I don't believe there was an estate. I got the feeling he was inventing the line about an estate. He was very vague about the details. My manager became suspicious and asked him to leave. He objected and I intervened.'

'Intervened, how?'

'I simply told him we were currently too busy to provide valuations on unseen works, and he left with the girl. I haven't seen them since.'

'Weston claims Miss Bunting visited your gallery a second time. Is that true?'

'Not to my knowledge Constable Parker.' Scarlet shrugged and glanced at what Parker suspected was a large Rolex watch, giving the impression he was short of time, and that he'd helped all he could.

Parker shifted her stance, scanned the gallery and tried to think of another question. She'd gleaned very little from the conversation apart from the feeling that Scarlet was a very smooth operator, as were many successful businessmen she'd interviewed.

'Is that all Constable?' Scarlet said, with a hint of impatience.

Parker nodded, thanked Scarlet for his cooperation and turned to leave.

'Boss, I'll feed the bitch again tonight...' Mullet cut his statement short when he spotted Parker's blue uniform from the office door behind Scarlet.

Scarlet's composure hardened around a fierce glare. Parker got a whiff of too much deodorant as Mullet scurried back toward the office at the back of the gallery, propelled by the pressure of Scarlet's glare. Parker also noticed Mullet's bandaged hand.

Parker flashed Scarlet a please explain eyebrow.

'Greyhound bitch. Terry, my gallery manager, trains a few greyhounds for me,' Scarlet said, deftly regaining his composure.

Parker nodded and left. Mullet certainly fitted the description of a stereotypical greyhound owner, but he most certainly did not fit that of a gallery manager.

On her return to Richmond station Senior Constable Parker began enquiries into any criminal connections Barry Scarlet might have in Europe.

Chapter Twenty-One

On the train into Richmond, Clay mulled over Red's comments about the attention he'd drawn by hiding out in the bathing box. If he didn't find Karen today, then he had no doubt his unusual digs would attract more than the odd drinker's attention. Either a council worker or a beach patrol might take an interest, which could eventually lead to police involvement.

Clay left Richmond Station and strode along Swan Street towards The Chicken Bar where the previous evening Mullet had bought takeaway. Clay headed for the hardware store further along, where he often purchased turps for cleaning brushes and timber to construct painting stretchers. The proprietor recognised him as an occasional customer and made no comment on Clay's purchase of bolt cutters, a short steel crowbar and canvas backpack: The perfect break-and-enter kit.

At about 9AM, Clay cautiously approached the vacant auto repair shop in Dover Street Mullet had entered on the previous night. The street was deserted, apart from cars parked bonnet to boot down the opposite side of the street. Their owners, who usually started work earlier, were employed by the light industrial businesses that had replaced some of the rundown single-fronted Victorian cottages common to this part of Richmond.

Clay didn't want to blunder into Mullet, so he loitered on the narrow footpath behind the parked cars and cased the auto shop from across the street. Clay watched the auto shop for a good ten minutes, before believing it was safe to approach and begin the break-in.

The bolt cutter sliced through the padlock securing the steel mesh gate he'd seen Mullet open on the previous night. Clay pushed the gate open and continued down the path to the timber panel side entrance door. An old deadlock secured this door. Clay tried the handle and found the door locked. He had no option but to force the door. Clay jammed the flat claw of the crowbar in between the jamb and the door stile, leant into the bar and forced them apart. At the same time, he reached down, turned the handle and shouldered hard against the door. On the second attempt, the door burst inwards.

Once inside, Clay unlatched the deadlock and pushed the door shut. Like his studio, which had once been a machinery shop, rows of overhead skylights allowed filtered light through pigeon shit and grime to softly light the interior. The smell of petrol, rubber and oil impregnating the stained concrete floor found Clay's nose. Clay tried the light switch just inside the door. No lights worked. The power was either turned off at the meter or disconnected.

As his eyes adjusted to the gloom, Clay could make out the shape of an elevated pneumatic car lift, over in front of the large sliding entrance doors. Some block and tackle chains hung down from overhead I-beams. Behind the lift, a pile of old tyres made a rubber sculpture that would have looked quite at home in the main exhibition room of the Victorian National Gallery. The rear brick wall was lined with rows of grimy wooden parts shelves, loaded with dusty automotive dross. A large, red-painted door centrally split the wall of shelves.

It was clear to Clay, that Karen had never been held in the main workshop because she could easily have yelled out loud enough to attract attention out front. She would have also heard him yelling and banging on the front sliding door the previous night. If Karen was imprisoned here, she had to be behind the red door.

Clay approached the door with the hope that the current mess he was in would soon be resolved. On the door, a faded white painted sign read FLAME STORE: a room-sized equivalent of the cabinet Clay was required to install in his own studio for flammable liquids such as turps and spray thinners.

A large steel sliding bolt secured the door. Clay dropped his bag of tools on the floor and rested the wrapped McCubbin he'd carried all the way from Brighton, up against the wall beside the red door. Clay grabbed the bolt with both hands and pulled. It slid back with a metallic scraping sound that put Clay's teeth on edge. Clay dragged the door open. It was easily as thick as his hand and constructed of fire bricks cemented into a welded steel support frame. It had to be soundproof.

The small room beyond was pitch black. A weak spray of light from the skylights behind Clay shafted into the room. At the same time, a dank smell of terpenes mixed with effluent, stale air and takeaway chicken wafted out. Clay could just make out a clump of blankets on top of an old mattress on the tiled floor against the far wall. Could Karen's lifeless body be under those blankets? Clay launched himself at the mattress, grabbed the blankets and cast them aside, to reveal nothing but a couple of pillows. Clay stared at the pillows and groaned, both relieved and disappointed at the same time.

A shadow flickered across his view, followed by a thudding pain at the back of his head. Clay sank onto the pillows and into blackness.

***

Clay opened his eyes to a vision blurred by spattered water. Pain blended with the sound of Karen's tremulous voice.

'Wake up. For God's sake, Clay, wake up.' Karen's voice reverberated around in Clay's skull like a bevy of Hitchcock's birds. 'I thought you were Mullet. God, I'm so sorry,' Karen said, kneeling beside him and squeezing water from a wet hand towel onto his face and forehead.

'What the hell did you hit me with?' Clay tentatively moved his head from side to side and gently prodded a rising egg on the back of his skull.

'Smashed a china cistern lid over your head.'

'For Christ's sake, you could have killed me!'

'That was the general idea.' Karen choked off a nervous giggle. 'But I lost my footing on the downswing.'

'Oh, very funny.'

'Well, you could say you fell for me,' she quipped.

Clay tried to smile, but his facial muscles were somehow connected with those at the back of his skull, and he ended up flinching instead.

'I've been waiting for fifteen minutes for you to wake up.'

'You could have gone for help. If you'd succeeded in crushing my skull, I'd need an ambulance.'

'No chance of that happening.'

'Why not? Is it against your Girl Guide code or something?' Clay stifled another painful smile.

'Can't leave. See?' Karen lifted a heavy dog chain that snaked along the floor. 'I'm chained to the back wall.' Clay could see one end attached to the plumbing pipes behind the toilet, and the other to a metal shackle around Karen's left ankle.

Karen stood up and did a barefoot shuffle over to a small hand basin on the opposite wall and dropped the hand towel over the rail beside it. The dog chain dragged along the tiled floor behind her. Karen's pale blue mini and matching blouse were crushed and stained with grime. At the basin, she cupped some water onto her face and examined her tangled hair in the cracked mirror over the basin. Clay realised, that even though the light entering from the open door was weak, it must have been the first time Karen had seen herself in hours. Karen gave up trying to sort out her hair and when she turned back to face Clay, he saw scratches down her forearms and the dark smudge of a bruise over her right eye.

'Bloody hell! Did Mullet do that to you? Mullet is an animal.!' Clay sat up and massaged the back of his neck.

The rising morning sun now provided enough light for Clay to see that the flammable liquids store they were in was once a restroom and may still have been used as such. The toilet bowl and cistern — now minus its lid — remained, along with a basin and mirror. The toilet stall walls had been removed to create extra room for volatile stores. It was the perfect prison cell.

Karen's chain was just long enough for her to reach the toilet and hand basin. A grimy towel now hung over the rail on the wall beside the hand basin. Most frighteningly for Karen, everything would have to be fumbled for in total darkness once the door was closed.

Clay climbed to his feet and headed out the door to get his bolt cutters.

'I'll make short work of that chain,' Clay said from beyond the door.

'Mullet's an animal all right,' Karen yelled out through the door. 'You should see the way he pervs on me. Creeps me out.'

When Clay failed to return immediately, Karen added. 'Hurry up, will you? I can't stand another minute in this filthy hole!'

Clay reappeared in the doorway, standing stiffly against the light and looked at Karen with oddly glazed eyes.

'Well, what are you doing, admiring the scenery?'

Clay lurched in, stumbled and fell to the floor in front of Karen with a moan.

'Mullet appeared behind in the doorway, a baseball-bat-sized length of two by three cradled in both hands.

'I'm the only animal round here who'll be doing any admirin', you mouthy bitch.'

Karen cringed but reached out and touched Clay's pale face.

'What have you done to him?'

Mullet's hacking laugh accompanied a kick into Clay's kidneys. 'A light tap on the neck with this 'ere lump of wood.'

Clay gave a muffled groan.

'You can give your nosey artist friend a cuddle while I figure out what I'm goin' to do with you both.' Mullet slammed the fire-door shut and pushed the bolt home.

Chapter Twenty-Two

Clay was sure he was conscious, his eyes wide open, but all he could see was blackness, a lamp black replete with an over glaze of rattling chains that Clay imagined came straight out of a horror film.

Karen stumbled into the back of Clay's head, and he jerked as his horror-film nightmare was augmented with a wave of pain.

'Shit! Sorry, Clay, I can't see a damn thing with the door closed.'

Clay moaned.

'Your poor head is having one hell of a day,' Karen said, her hands fumbling across Clay's face in the dark with the damp towel. 'Put this behind your head; it might help with the pain.'

Clay groaned and rolled over onto his knees and spread the wet cloth over the back of his neck. The pain in the back of his head was throbbing through to his forehead. Remembering how grotty the towel looked when he last saw it, Clay said, 'Knowing my luck, I'll probably catch cholera from this towel.'

'Nice to know my efforts are appreciated,' Karen said, placing an arm around Clay's waist and helping him to his feet.

'What's happened since I revisited the land of nod?' Clay asked, beginning to appreciate Karen's arm around his waist.

'Nothing. You can't hear shit when the door is shut in this hole. I guess he's trying to figure out what to do with us.'

Together they shuffled towards the back wall like a couple of kids in a three-legged race, feeling for the edge of the mattress with their feet.

'I suspect Mullet makes very few decisions on his own. My bet is, he's gone to consult with Scarlet,' Clay said, as they both sank down upon the mattress. 'Doesn't look good though. If they let us go, then their game is up the minute we go to the police. The police may not believe me, but they sure as hell will believe you after you tell them how you were abducted and imprisoned.'

They sat silently in the dark, straining to hear through the fire door. Clay moved the damp towel to his forehead, and Karen reached out in the dark to rub the back of Clay's neck.

Clay's head still ached, but the press of Karen's bare thigh against him, and her gentle massaging of the back of his neck, were doing wonders.

'How'd you get the bruised eye?' Clay asked, trying to reciprocate Karen's concern for his head.

'I gave Mullet a hard time when he showed up at my flat. Didn't you see the little prick's bandaged hand? I did that when I kicked him in the groin, and he doubled over and fell through my five-hundred-dollar Noguchi glass coffee table.'

'I saw your flat; it looked like Cyclone Tracy had re-arranged the interior.'

'Yeah. Not the kind of redecorating Pam and I had in mind.

When I confronted those two arseholes at B.S. Fine Art the second time, I was pretty angry. I threatened to go to the police. I was bluffing of course; I didn't have any evidence. Scarlet claimed he couldn't even remember Pam applying for the hostess job.'

'Scarlet's a cool customer,' Clay said, turning to let Karen work his neck with both hands. 'He's the brains. Mullet's just the muscle.'

'Muscle! You've got to be joking. I nearly got the better of him at my flat until he clocked me with my not-so-expensive Ikea floor lamp. That's how I got this shiner. My visit must have scared them enough to come after me.' Karen stopped massaging and said, 'Clay, I think we need a plan for when Mullet returns.'

When Clay didn't immediately jump in with a suggestion, Karen continued. 'Hell, if you hadn't shoved your head into my escape plan, we wouldn't be in this trouble.'

'Oh really, I apologise on my head's behalf.'

'We should be able to take him out. For starters, you're almost twice the size of that little runt, and besides, there are two of us.'

'Well, you're pretty good with ambushes. What do you suggest?'

'I dunno, maybe you could get up against the wall beside the door like I did with you. When he comes in, I'll distract him, and you take him down with a body tackle.'

'Mullet might be dumb, but he won't be as easy as I was. He'll be expecting something like that.'

'Come on Clay, you're supposed to be the creative one. Think of somethi —.'

—The scrape of the bolt being withdrawn interrupted Karen. They both stood back up and waited. Karen whispered, 'Give me a nod when you're going to jump him.'

The door swung open, and Mullet stood silhouetted in the opening. For an instant, Clay thought about rushing the little man, but as his eyes adjusted to the light, the glint of a long metal blade in Mullet's hand restrained him.

Mullet sounded tense.

'Come on, art-man, do me a favour. Run into my blade.'

Clay took a deep breath of the slightly sweeter air seeping in from the garage, thinking that some extra oxygen might help clear his head.

'Step forward into the light and turn around and get down on your knees with your hands behind your back,' Mullet demanded, pointing at the concrete floor with his blade.

'What, so you can cut my throat? I'd rather tackle you straight up,' Clay said, edging forward.

'No need to play the 'ero for your girlfriend, art-man. I only wanna tie your hands. Can't have you runnin' around loose in this 'ere garage like a stock car in a demolition derby.'

Mullet's wheezing laugh at his own joke matured into a coughing fit. When Mullet's coughing had subsided, he said, 'Now do as you're told, or I'll be forced to cut your girlfriend.'

Clay glared at Mullet. 'If you hurt Karen, I swear...'

'Oh, give the artist an Oscar,' Mullet wheezed before raising his voice to a rattling squeal. 'Now do as you're fuckin' told!'

Clay looked over at Karen and their eyes negotiated a silent accord to act on Karen's suggested plan at the first opportunity. Clay turned back to Mullet and complied by slowly turning, kneeling and placing his hands behind his back.

Mullet sneered with satisfaction. At the same time, he threw a length of greasy nylon rope onto the floor in front of Karen.

'Ok bitch, tie your boyfriend's wrists together as tightly as you can with one end, then wrap the remainder of the rope around his waist so he can't move his arms.'

Karen did as she was told. When she'd finished, Mullet waved her away with his blade, then he advanced into the room, checked the tightness of the rope, dragged Clay to his feet and pushed him out into the auto shop. Clay's head throbbed with each step. Mullet pushed Clay toward two dusty office chairs placed back-to-back in the centre of the shop. Mullet pushed Clay into one of the chairs and padlocked him to the chair with a length of heavy chain. When Clay was secure, Mullet went back to the flame store and returned a moment later, pushing a reluctant Karen, her dog chain still dragging from her ankle, toward the other chair. Mullet wrapped the lighter chain around Karen and the chair, securing the free end with the padlock from the flame store.

Clay judged the time to be almost noon by the angle of the sunlight streaming in through the skylights. When Clay looked up at the skylights, he also noticed that their two chairs were positioned directly under a clutch of gently swaying V8 engine blocks roped together.

Mullet had been a busy boy, while he and Karen plotted in the silent isolation of the flame store. Mullet had hoisted three old engine blocks high into the roof trusses with one of the auto shop's block and tackles that ran along an I-beam. The weight of the engine blocks was now taken by strung-together lengths of old seatbelt webbing, which Mullet had scrounged from the automotive detritus that littered the garage. Clay's eye followed the path of the straining webbing, which ran over the I-beam to angle down and be tied off at the nearest metal support on the car lift.

Mullet noticed the direction of Clay's interest and grinned.

'Like my handiwork?' Mullet crowed, placing both hands on his hips and trying unsuccessfully to inflate his anaemic chest. Clay didn't answer what appeared to be Mullet congratulating himself. Mullet paced around his two captives, cat chattering to himself, before dragging another chair from the shadows along one wall of the workshop.

'Right.' Mullet placed the chair so that both Clay and Karen could see him. 'I don't know how you managed to find this bitch, art-man. But since you 'ave, I'll 'ave to adjust Barry's plan to stitch you up for the demise of yet another of your girlies.'

'Demise! You make murder sound like death by natural causes.' Clay gave Mullet a fierce look.

'Was that first bitch's own fault. She should've kept 'er nose out of our business,' Mullet said, attempting to sound like the victim.

'Art forgery and fraud is not a legitimate business Mullet,' Clay said wriggling on his chair to test his ropes.

Mullet sniggered at Clay until he choked on a gob of phlegm, which he spat at Clay's feet. His throat clear, Mullet continued. 'Who said anything about a legit business?' Mullet gave both Clay and Karen a grimy grin, pulled a pack of smokes from his jacket pocket, extracted a cigarette and lit up. 'We gave your porno model the bloody job at the gallery, an' she goes an' snoops around in Barry's office. Then gets all 'igh and mighty and quits the job the minute we catch her.'

'Ahh, so Pamela was on to your dodgy game?' Clay said, trying to keep Mullet talking long enough for his battered brain to suggest a way out of their predicament.

'That's what Barry reckoned. That's why he had me put the frighteners on the bitch.' Mullet sucked in a lung full of smoke and held it in until it seemed to seep out his eyes and ears. 'I followed her pink Bambino down to your digs and 'ung 'round for hours waitin' for that bitch to leave so I could have a little chat with her. Then, instead of 'er leavin', you did.' Mullet pointed a bony nicotine-stained finger at Clay.

Karen sat silently gaping at Mullet, her small hands fisted and white-knuckled with rage.

'I knocks on the door and she opens it. Surprised 'er, I did. Not as much as she surprised me, standin' there with her tit hanging out of that short black Japanesie thing she was 'ardly wearin'. Said she thought it was art-man 'ere, comin' back for his keys.'

'You horrible ugly grot!' Karen spat; her sudden utterance laced with anger. Mullet took a final drag and snarled through the exhaled smoke, 'Mmm... you're another feisty bitch, just like your sexy model friend.' Mullet leered at Karen, leaving little doubt about his intentions.

Karen shrank back into her chains, with a look of horror etched on her face.

Mullet stood up, lit another cigarette from the stub of the previous one, and began to pace around his captives continuing to recount his grim narration of events.

'After I made it clear to your porno model that she 'ad to keep her trap shut, what does she do? She doesn't say, yes, sir I'll keep my mouth shut. Oh no, instead she goes an' gets all uppity. Tries to push me out of the place. Mind you, while she's doing this she's half out of her fuckin' wrap thing.'

Mullet paused to expel another gob of phlegm before taking a further deep drag on his rapidly depleting cigarette.

Clay looked on, hoping Mullet would either pass out from smoke inhalation or collapse into a cancerous pile of gunk. A wild hope that was unlikely to happen. If he and Karen were to escape this mess, it would need to be due to their own efforts.

'I don't take no bitch pushin' me around, so I slaps her across the chops and pushes her back. Stops her cold for a second. But now she's standin' there with her wrap hanging fully open, giving me an eyeful. Does she cover-up? No sir, not her. Instead, she gets even feistier and comes at me punchin', kickin' and scratchin'. So, I grabs her round the throat. But she keeps on like a bloody stuck record, hitting and kicking like a psyched-out Thai boxer. I had no choice but to squeeze an' to shut the stupid bitch up.'

'No choice?' Karen gasped, through a strangled sob. 'You always have a choice. You're just too fucking dumb to know. You can't blame poor innocent Pamela for your murderous behaviour.'

Mullet's sullen expression showed how much he hated Karen's remarks. Clay thought it best to keep Mullet distracted, in the hope that any delay might provide an escape opportunity.

'Tell me, Terry,' Clay said soothingly, 'What did you do with Pam's body? Because she wasn't in my studio when I returned early next morning.'

'Not really your business, art-man, but since you won't be around to blab, there's no 'arm you knowin'.

I bundled her into the boot of Barry's Jag. Barry wasn't too 'appy, but when you two geezers turns up the next morning askin' about the girl, Barry figured we could dump her so as to put you in the frame,' Mullet said, pointing a nicotine-stained finger at Clay.

'It was simple. I went straight back to your digs, slipped the lock, grabbed the porno paintin' and the bitch's clothes and dumps her with the painting in a waste bin in that lane behind your studio. What's it called?'

'Little Cotton Way,' Clay muttered, despondently.

'Yeah, that's the place,' Mullet said sounding pleased. 'Right beside that stupid pink Italian pimple car of hers.' Mullet chortled through exhaled smoke after each revelation, strutting about proudly like a boss cocky.

Clay could hear Karen's chain grating against her chair as she strained with anger.

'Barry's plan worked like a trick. A quick call to the coppers and art-man's name is all over the news. Then to top it off, we discover he's pissed off. Dropped yourself right in the shit, didn't you?' Mullet's grin reminded Clay of the madmen depicted in Goya's Black Paintings.

Karen groaned, 'God, I'm sorry Clay. I went to the police when you didn't ring me and told them you were the last person to see Pamela.'

'It's okay Karen. At the time I didn't know what was going on. I knew I wasn't involved in Pamela's disappearance, so I went to Sydney...'

A sudden explosion of Mullet's wheezing laughter drowned out Clay and Karen's commiserations.

Clay squirmed at the sound.

Mullet skulked over to Karen and fondled her hair. Karen shrank back. 'You see,' Mullet boasted. 'I chose this place carefully. The police are goin' to think that lover boy 'ere,' Mullet glowered in the direction of Clay, 'snatched the pretty friend of his nudie model and locked her in this abandoned garage - which just 'appens to back right on to 'is Little Cotton Way porn studio - all arranged so he could 'ave his evil way with her. But things go bad, and you both die in an unfortunate accident, when these engine blocks fall —'

'— No one's going to believe that we just happened to be under these...' Clay nodded in the direction of the suspended engine blocks. 'Was this Scarlet's idea?'

'Nope. All my own work.' Mullet crowed. 'My take on Barry's original plan, to dispose of your nudie girl.'

Clay stared wide-eyed, struck by the naive stupidity of Mullet's plan, but he also now realised that Mullet's revelation provided an opportunity to delay the inevitable.

'Barry won't be pleased when he discovers he's missed out on over half a million dollars,' Clay said, closely watching for Mullet's reaction.

'What the 'ell is you talkin' about?' Mullet said, losing interest in Karen's hair, to Karen's obvious relief.

'Oh, so you didn't notice the beach towel wrapped parcel leaning against the wall next to the flame store door?'

Mullet stepped away from Karen and peered across the garage in the direction of the flame store. 'No. What is it?'

'A painting. I was going to have Barry Scarlet value it this afternoon after I'd helped Karen.' This was a calculated lie that Clay hoped would confuse Mullet. 'He's expecting me.'

'He's expecting you?' Mullet parroted, his head oscillating between the package and his captives.

'Yep, he sure is. And if you dispose of us now, you'll have to dispose of the painting as well. The painting's ownership, its provenance, is connected to me and couldn't suddenly turn up in Scarlet's possession without questions being asked.' Clay could see by Mullet's dancing eyes that he was trying hard to process this new information. Clay continued to press this meagre advantage. 'Maybe you should check with Barry before you do anything rash. I'm sure he'd be as mad as hell to miss out on all that money. Maybe we could do a deal. The painting for our silence.' The silence that followed Clay's offer was punctuated only by Mullet's uncertain wheezy breathing.

There was an obvious flaw in Clay's argument. Mullet could still kill them and take the painting to his boss, who could no doubt find a private buyer. But Clay had witnessed Mullet cringe whenever Scarlet stepped in to tidy up after his tantrums at B.S Fine Art. Clay hoped that Mullet's fear of Scarlet would pressure him to consult Scarlet, thus giving him and Karen time.

Mullet tentatively approached the package.

'It's not a bomb, it's only a painting.' Clay said, with an offhand laugh.

Mullet grunted, prodded the painting with his foot, picked it up and stripped off the beach towel. He turned the painting to catch the light. 'How much did you say this is worth?'

'It's a McCubbin, must be worth close to a million dollars. A couple of years ago, Bush Idyll, a larger painting by the same artist was indemnified by the Australian Government for a touring exhibition for nearly three million dollars. I'm sure Barry would know about that,' Clay said, with every ounce of chutzpa he could muster.

Mullet acknowledged each mention of money with a grunt, and then quite suddenly, he loosely rewrapped the painting and headed for the side entrance.

'Stay put.' Mullet guffawed at what he'd just said and left.

When the door slammed behind Mullet, Karen breathed a sigh of relief.

'Christ Clay, that was magic. You almost had me believing all that bullshit.'

'It's not total bull Karen. Remember the fake painting scheme we cooked up with Julia. Well, that's the fake painting. I arranged to deliver the picture to Julia today, because Julia arranged for Scarlet to value it.'

'I thought you'd given up on that plan,' Karen said, her voice still registering her antipathy to the idea. 'Still, bullshit or not, you gained us a reprieve.'

'Only a minor reprieve Karen. I figure, that if we're still here when Mullet returns, we may have made things worse if Scarlet gets involved.'

'Then we have to get out of here,' Karen said, taking a deep breath and combing her fingers through her hair. 'Did you see how that weasel was touching me. So, yuck.'

'Yeah, I know. Let's try something before he gets back. Can you reach the knot in this rope tying my hands and arms down?'

Clay felt Karen's cold hands fumbling over his constrained arms as they squirmed for the best position for her to access the knot. In any other circumstance he'd have enjoyed her touch.

Chapter Twenty-Three

'I think I've undone the knot,' Karen said, after five minutes picking and pulling. 'But I can't see how it's going to help; you're still chained to that bloody chair.'

'Yes, but my arms are now free.' Clay waved his arms about like a naval signaller. 'Mullet was so fixated on telling Scarlet about the painting, he rushed out and forgot the bolt cutters in my bag of break-in tools,' Clay pointed to his canvas backpack lying on the floor beside the flame store door. 'All we have to do is hop our chairs over there and we can cut our chains free.'

'How long have we got?' Karen said, starting to hop her chair.

'My guess is not long. The nearest public phone is at Richmond Station, which is no more than ten minutes' walk.' Clay took the lead with a couple of long dangerous chair hops. 'Ten minutes there, ten back and ten minutes talking to Scarlet. I'd say we have half an hour, maximum.'

'Is Mullet on foot?'

'I don't think he has his own car. When I followed him here the other night, he used the train.' Clay was making good progress with big hops. 'Also, he said he was driving Scarlet's Jag the night he dropped by my studio to murder Pamela.'

Karen stopped to watch Clay. Suddenly horrified to see him teetering on the edge of falling, after a reckless hop.

'Hey! Take it easy Clay. If you fall over in that chair, I doubt I'll be able to help you up.'

'I reckon I could almost drag myself along the floor to the bag, now my arms are free,' Clay said, regaining his balance and somewhat elated at the nearness of the canvas backpack, which was now only three metres away. Karen renewed hopping her chair in Clay's direction and after about ten minutes of frantic jumping they both managed to rendezvous at the bag.

Clay manoeuvred his chair into position and cut through the dog chain that was wrapped around Karen. He cut through the small padlock securing her metal ankle cuff. Karen danced around in front of Clay, delighted to be free, and then seizing the remnants of the chain and metal cuff, she threw them into the flame store.

'Right, now I'll get to work on your chain,' Karen said, taking the bolt-cutters from Clay.

'You will have to cut through the padlock, Karen. My chain isn't a dog chain, it's heavier; the padlock is the weakest link.'

'We were chained up by the missing link,' Karen said, laughing as she circled around behind Clay to get at his padlock.

'Can you get to it?' Clay said, trying to peer over his shoulder.

'Yep, I've got the cutters on it right now, but it's bloody hard.'

'Grip the bolt cutters by the ends of the handles, you'll get more leverage.'

'I am. I'm not stupid!' Karen said, grunting with frustration.

'What the fuck!'

Clay's head snapped around in the direction of Mullet's voice. Mullet was almost upon them; he'd quietly entered the auto shop while they were preoccupied with escape. Karen kept frantically working at Clay's padlock.

Mullet rushed at them. He swung a round-arm punch at Karen, who turned away just in time to take the blow on her shoulder. Karen staggered back but managed a swing at Mullet with the bolt cutters. Off balance, Karen's wild swing failed to connect. Clay jump-dragged his chair towards the flame store, his arms flailing for Mullet. Karen backed up into the doorway of the flame store, with Mullet cautiously advancing on her. As Mullet moved closer, he pulled out the flick knife he'd threatened Clay with earlier. Karen's eyes widened to look like those of a Manga comic character. Although clearly terrified, Karen lined Mullet up and hurled the heavy bolt cutters at him, just as Clay dragged on a handful of Mullet's coat. The bolt cutters missed Mullet's head by inches but grazed the right side of Clay's head. Clay fell backwards in a clatter of chains and chair.

Karen took a step back in shock; she'd nearly killed Clay again.

Mullet pressed his advantage, jumped forward, slammed the flame store door shut and pushed the bolt home, trapping Karen inside. With Karen secured, he turned his attention to Clay, who lay on his side, dazed and still firmly chained to his chair, a thin trickle of blood running down the right side of his face.

'I should cut your fuckin' nose off!' Mullet screamed at Clay. Clay did not respond; he only groaned each time Mullet sank his boot into his kidneys. Eventually, Mullet's pathetic fitness resulted in his kicking giving way to a coughing fit.

When Mullet regained his composure, he grabbed the back of Clay's chair and dragged him upright. Clay glared at Mullet as he wiped the trickle of blood from his face with the back of his hand.

'I'd finish you off right now if I 'ad my way.' Mullet said, depositing a gob of spit onto the leg of Clay's jeans. 'But Barry wants a word with you about that painting. After that, you're both my problem to deal with.'

Clay smiled inwardly. The painting was still working for them.

'Barry's coming here, is he?'

'When he's ready.' Mullet replied, skittishly pacing back and forth in front of Clay's chair.

'Drag yourself back where you were, under the engines.'

Clay stayed put, staring defiantly back up at Mullet.

'Fuckin' move!' Mullet screamed, pulling out his switchblade and thrusting it in front of Clay's face. 'You only need to be alive to answer Barry's questions.'

Clay could see fear and unease in Mullet's eyes. Clay figured Mullet's chat with Scarlet had not gone well. Clay thought it best to comply and wait for another opportunity to get the better of Mullet. However, the urgency to act had increased now that Scarlet was involved. Clay suspected Scarlet might be an even greater threat.

Feigning cooperation, Clay hopped his chair back in the direction of the precariously suspended engine blocks. Clay did not like the idea of sitting directly under that mass of metal, but with Mullet's nervous jabbing with his knife, Clay felt it unwise to object.

'How long before Scarlet gets here?' Clay asked, again trying to diffuse the obvious tension evident in Mullet's behaviour.

'I told you. He'll get 'ere when he's fuckin' ready,' Mullet's curt response again showed his fear at Scarlet's involvement. Clay chose not to press the point; instead, he turned his attention back to the engine blocks suspended overhead. Clay traced the path of the strung-together seatbelt straps, which supported the weighty threat, back to the tie-off point at the hoist support.

Periodically, the straps issued a strained creak. It was not these unsettling sounds that attracted Clay's attention, but the hatchet Clay had not previously noted, leaning against the hoist support. Mullet noticed the direction of Clay's attention and revitalised by his obvious power over Clay, grinned knowingly, pocketing his flick knife in favour of another cigarette. Mullet circled back toward the fire store door, gathered up the nylon rope Karen had untied and used it to tie Clay's chair to a steel D-ring anchor set in the workshop floor near his chair.

'That should keep you from frog-hopping around while I deal with your girlfriend.'

'She's no threat to you, locked in the flame store,' Clay said, worried by Mullet's move towards the flame store.

'Yes, you're right, art-hole,' Mullet sneered at Clay. 'But Barry told me she was my problem. And I intend to have some fun with the feisty bitch before I eliminate that problem.'

'Leave her alone, you slimy prick!' Clay strained and jerked futilely against his chains.

Mullet gave a gurgling laugh at Clay's protestations, cleared his tortured throat by spitting, threw his dead cigarette aside and drew back the flame store bolt. Pulling out his flick knife Mullet pulled open the door.

'Coming, ready or not, girly.' Mullet advanced cautiously into the gloomy store; knife extended.

Clay held his breath, stunned by his inability to help. He heard no sound from Karen. Mullet disappeared from Clay's view. After a few seconds, a crunching thwack broke the silence, followed by a howl of pain from inside the flame store.

'Fuckin' bitch!' howled Mullet.

A moment later, Karen burst from the flame store, the dog chain looped to form a Medieval flail with the steel ankle cuff swinging dangerously. Karen veered sharply right as she left the store, flattening herself against the wall of the flame store.

'Karen's got some pluck,' Clay thought when he realised her intention to ambush Mullet again rather than run from him.

Mullet appeared at the entrance, his face contorted with pain and anger, his right hand clearly injured, hung lacerated and limp, the knife now in his left hand. He stared out across the auto shop looking for Karen. Too late he realised that she was still close by, winding up for a second attack.

The steel chain and cuff whirred through the God beams filtering down from the skylights to smash into the side of Mullet's head. Mullet screamed with pain. A red gash appeared across his face. Karen did not quit; she danced around Mullet flailing him about the head and neck without mercy. The chain dislodged his knife, which skittered away across the concrete floor. Mullet tried to protect his head with his arms, but Karen redirected her attack at his legs, which soon buckled.

Mullet collapsed into a moaning foetal huddle on the concrete floor. Karen stopped belting into Mullet and stepped back, her chest heaving from the adrenalin-fuelled exertion.

Mullet appeared to be semi-conscious. Blood seeped from several lacerations inflicted by the cuff on Mullet's exposed skin. His pants were torn about the knees, and Clay had no doubt that painful welts and bruises would be forming across his legs and back.

Karen stared at Mullet, the bloodied chain swinging with merciless intent from her blood-spattered hand. For a moment, Clay feared that the instant Karen regained her breath, she would continue her attack, but she hesitated unsure what to do next. Clay took the opportunity to engage Karen.

'Over here, Karen. Untie this rope. You can use it to secure Mullet.'

Karen looked across at Clay bewildered, but after a few seconds, she nodded and trotted over to where Clay was restrained. In shock, Karen was incapable of speech and stood confused and inert beside Clay.

'Untie the rope holding my chair in place,' Clay said, gently directing Karen. 'Then take it over and tie Mullet's hands and feet together while he's disabled.'

'Uh-hm,' Karen said, dropping the chain and setting to work on the rope knots.

'Remind me not to pick an argument with you,' Clay said, making light of their situation to allay Karen's state of shock. Karen stayed focused on loosening Clay's ropes. Clay had seen Karen's shocked reaction before when they'd had their first violent encounter with Mullet at B.S. Fine Art. He knew she would eventually surface, and he hoped she would soon snap back with her usual assertive confidence.

Karen soon had the ropes untied, and with Clay's urging, she moved over to where Mullet silently lay in the same crumpled position on the concrete floor, just outside the flame store.

Karen gave Mullet a cautious kick to gauge his responsiveness. He appeared to be unconscious. Karen bent over Mullet and pulled at his arm to access his hands.

Suddenly, Clay noticed Karen's abandoned chain weapon lying on the floor beside him and with a warning shout still forming in his throat, Clay saw Mullet's good hand fly out and clamp onto Karen's neck. Karen fell on top of Mullet. Each struggled to get the advantage.

Horrified, Clay watched the tussle. He was still chained to the seat, arms free and able to hop about but essentially helpless. Apparently, most of the injuries Karen had earlier inflicted on Mullet were superficial, and although he was a small man, he was still capable of overpowering Karen. Although dazed by shock, Karen fought hard enough to break free from Mullet's stranglehold. She stood up and staggered across the workshop towards Clay.

'Grab the chain!' Clay yelled, pointing at her discarded chain weapon lying beside his chair.

Karen moved to reclaim the chain, but Mullet was quickly on his feet following, spraying curses. When Karen stopped and bent to retrieve the chain from the floor near Clay, Mullet caught hold of her hair and swung her away from the weapon. Karen collided with Clay, tumbling over him onto the floor. Mullet's arms were flailing for Karen like an enraged malfunctioning automaton. Intent on his pursuit of Karen, Mullet blundered into Clay.

'Got you!' Clay yelled, grabbing hold of Mullet from behind with his free arms. Clay's bear hug trapped both Mullet's arms to his sides and had Mullet sitting in Clay's lap. Clay's arms, developed from years of paddling his surfboard, squeezed hard around Mullet's chest, pushing the air out of his feeble lungs.

'Fuck you, art boy,' Mullet wheezed. With his ribs at cracking point, Mullet slammed his head back into Clay's face. Blood spurted from Clay's nose, but he hung on and increased the pressure on Mullet, avoiding further head butts by moving his head left and right. Mullet howled with angry frustration.

'Karen, Grab the hatchet and cut the strap holding the engine blocks,' Clay yelled!

Karen looked up at Clay not understanding what he wanted.

'Over beside the hoist,' Clay said nodding in the direction of the hoist. 'I can't hold this greasy little turd forever.'

Mention of the hatchet motivated Mullet to struggle with renewed vigour.

Now a life-or-death struggle, Mullet began jumping up and down in Clay's lap, occasionally managing to scrape the heel of his shoe down Clay's shin.

Karen dragged herself across the floor to the hoist and grabbed the hatchet.

'Hurry, Karen! Cut the strap. I can't hold him much longer.'

'What about you!' Karen screamed standing up. 'They will crush you too. Why don't I try and clobber him with the hatchet?' Karen pleaded swaying unsteadily.

'No time!' Clay gasped, blood streaming down his face from another head butt to the nose.

'Do it, don't worry about me.'

At that moment, Mullet managed to get an arm free, and he started pounding Clay's side with his elbow.

The sight of Mullet breaking free impelled Karen to act. She swung the hatchet down hard on the seat-belt strapping, the first strike only partly severing the belt. The engine blocks dropped an inch, and the belt retook the strain.

Mullet glanced up at the blocks swaying overhead.

'Stupid bitch!' Mullet screamed. 'You're only goin' to kill your fuckin' boyfriend.'

'He's not my boyfriend, you dumb shit!' Karen slammed the hatchet down on the remaining strand of webbing.

The webbing gave way with a dull twang and the engines fell.

Clay pushed Mullet forward and with the last of his remaining energy hopped his chair backward. Mullet tried to redirect Clay's push by diving to the left, but the engines slammed down pinning Mullet's right leg with a bone-splintering crunch.

Clay's chair arced backwards, causing his head to hit the concrete floor, spinning Clay into unconsciousness.

Chapter Twenty-Four

Clay groaned, his eyelids fluttered up and down a few times and then remained open. He was no longer chained to the chair. In the background, Clay could hear a plaintive whine punctuated by the occasional moan.

'How's your head?' Karen asked, cradling Clay's bruised head in her lap while gently dabbing his brow with the wet towel.

'Is that Mullet I can hear blubbering?' Clay asked, lifting an arm to shade his eyes from a skylight's pale beam, which felt like a welding flash.

'Yeah. I think his leg is badly crushed,' Karen said. 'He's pinned under that clutch of engines. I haven't lifted a finger to help him.'

Laughing intensified the pain in Clay's head, so he opted for a weak smile. 'Did you use the bolt cutters on my chain?'

'No. I went through that slime ball's pockets and found the key. I kicked him in his bad leg every time he even looked like moving.'

'You're almost back to your old self,' Clay said, with a grin.

'I've had some time. You've been out cold for twenty minutes. I was getting worried that Scarlet might turn up. I thought, if you didn't come around soon, I'd have to leave and try to get help. Then you groaned and started to move your legs, so I put some water on that filthy towel from the flame store. I wasn't sure which would kill you first, the towel or the knock on the head. But now that you're awake, let's get the hell out of here.' Karen lifted Clay's head from her lap and stood up. Clay's head tapped the floor. He gave a small yelp. 'Your poor head has certainly taken a beating today,' Karen said, pacing about waiting for Clay to pull himself together.

'You can't leave me 'ere like this. I need 'elp,' Mullet whined.

'Did you hear a noise, Clay? I think it must be rats,' Karen said heading for the door.

'You fuckin' bitch!' Mullet screamed; his pleading tone gone.

'Hang on, Karen, let me grab my tools.' Clay gathered up his backpack, and a moment later he found the fake McCubbin leaning against the wall near the side entrance.

Karen was already at the door waiting. As Clay moved to join Karen, he called to Mullet, 'Scarlet should be here soon. I'm sure his Workers' Compensation Insurance will cover your injuries.' Clay allowed himself a laugh despite the jabbing pain it triggered in his head. Clay cast an admiring eye over the painting before stuffing it in his backpack and opting for one final verbal jab at Mullet before leaving he said, 'Just thought I should remind you that you will now also have to explain the loss of the McCubbin to Scarlet.' Clay opened the door.

'That's very interesting Mr. Weston. Now back up you two.' Scarlet stood framed in the doorway, his tailored Italian suit shining almost as much as the silver pistol pointed at Clay's chest.

Karen's eyes rolled skyward, and she sighed with exasperation. They both backed away slowly. Clay couldn't believe their bad luck. How many times did they need to attempt to escape? Scarlet followed them into the workshop. From beneath the engines, Mullet gave a gurgling laugh of triumph, which did not totally disguise his latent fear.

'Thank God you're here. I was dealing with these two troublemakers just before you arrived, Barry.'

Scarlet directed Clay and Karen to lie face down side by side on the concrete floor in front of the incapacitated Mullet. He kept his pistol firmly trained on them.

'Lying down on the job Terry?' Scarlet said, without the slightest hint of humour.

'No boss. It was a mistake. My leg is badly broke. I need 'elp.'

'Yes Terry, you do need help. I'm afraid I was under the mistaken impression that you could be trusted to clean up this situation. And what do I discover? Firstly, you turn up at my business with that gallery hostess's body in the trunk of my Mercedes, forcing me to do some serious thinking to deflect police attention. And now, you compound that initial mistake by abducting her girlfriend — something I did not authorise. I only find out about it, when you decide to ring me about some supposedly valuable painting. And guess what Terry? The first thing I hear when I walk in here is, that that valuable painting is nowhere to be seen.'

'Yes, but Barry it's all sorted now you're 'ere. Right?'

'Yeah, you're right Terry. Now that I am here, I will have to sort it.'

'Sort it soon please, Barry, 'cause I'm in terrible pain, I might need to go to 'ospital.'

'All in good time Terry, all in good time,' Scarlet replied offhandedly, turning his attention to Clay and Karen.

'Now. You two have become a significant nuisance,' Scarlet said, waving his pistol at his prone captives.

'I'm sorry we've been an inconvenience,' Clay replied, 'but you shouldn't have killed our friend Pamela.'

'Mmmm. As you heard. Not my desired outcome, but a problematic outcome nonetheless.' Scarlet pointed at Clay's backpack. 'What's in the bag?'

'The McCubbin Mullet phoned you about, and some tools,' Clay said, happy to reveal the painting and change the subject.

'Show me the painting.'

Clay sat up and opened the backpack and emptied the contents onto the concrete floor. Scarlet stepped forward, picked up the painting and kicked the bolt cutters and crowbar to one side, away from Clay, motioning for Clay to lie back down. He then moved to examine the painting in a shaft of light from one of the skylights, occasionally interrupting his examination to check on Clay and Karen. When he'd finished, he smiled and stepped closer to Clay.

'Not bad. It's a very good painting. In fact, I suspect this might be the same McCubbin that Julia Blakely arranged for me to value later this afternoon. I now realise that you, Mr. Weston, are one of Blakely's stable of artists and that you have both conspired, you might say, cooked up a little scheme to incriminate me. Set me up for the police, so to speak, eh?'

'See, Barry? That's why I had to ring you,' Mullet implored, between whimpers of pain.

'Told you it was a dumb idea,' Karen whispered into Clay's ear.

Clay lifted his head from the concrete floor to grin at Scarlet. Behind the grin he was terrified.

'You're right, that is the painting you were to value. And you are correct in assuming it was part of a ploy to expose your fraudulent business. I'm almost certain that you've been selling fakes at B.S. Fine Art ever since your gallery opened.' Clay paused searching for an angle that might unsettle Scarlet. 'You should also realise, that because I haven't delivered the painting to Julia, she is probably wondering where I am, and is more than likely contacting the police right now.'

Scarlet lifted an eyebrow,

'Only probably? You don't sound too certain Mr. Weston,' Scarlet kept his pistol aimed at Clay as he backed away to carefully place the painting against a pallet of old tyres stacked behind him. 'Your girlfriend is right, Mr Weston,' Scarlet continued, sidling over to where he'd kicked the contents of Clay's backpack. 'Your ploy was a dumb idea, because, if you had blown my business cover and compromised my operation, then you'd leave me with few options.' Scarlet paused, bent down and picked up the bolt cutters. He hefted them in his left hand and smiled, 'I guess I need to start cleaning up a few loose ends.'

Scarlet pocketed his pistol and strode up to Clay and Karen, stepping over them and on towards Mullet. Mullet stopped mewling and gave Scarlet a wan smile as he approached. Scarlet beamed a consoling smile, grabbed the heavy bolt cutters with both hands, lifted them overhead and slammed them down in between Mullet's incredulous eyes.

At the sickening sound of crushing skull bone, Clay felt Karen flinch beside him, taking short fearful gasps of air and shaking. Clay realised that Karen was probably retreating into shock again and would be unlikely to be able to help if they had to confront Scarlet. He was starting to think he should have gone straight to the police when he suspected where Karen was being held. Clay's blood ran cold with the realisation that he would have to do some fast thinking and talking if they were to avoid being killed by Scarlet.

Scarlet threw the bolt cutters onto the mess of body, blood and engines, retrieved the pistol from his pocket and coolly walked back to confront Clay and Karen.

'Lucky for you, Weston, I don't believe that Julia has involved the police. When I spoke with her this morning about the valuation, she claimed that the Mc-Cubbin was from a deceased estate Karen Bunting had acquired. The same collection you mentioned the first time you visited B.S. Fine Art.

Having seen the painting now, I believe it to be genuine. I also believe that Julia Blakely would not risk Blakely Gallery's reputation by involving the police during a valuation of a work she was representing. Also, as it is now late afternoon if your claim of police involvement was true, then we should all be knee-deep in blue uniforms by now.'

Clay could not believe his ears. He wondered why it was that crooks always needed to explain their thinking to their victims, but he kept quiet because the longer Scarlet ranted the longer, they survived.

'Sadly, for you,' Scarlet continued. 'I still have to clean up the mess that idiot Mullet created —'

'— Mr. Scarlet. Can I call you Barry?' Clay finessed before Scarlet could complete what Clay feared he was about to say. 'Clearly, you have correctly assessed that Julia was testing your bona fides as a valuer and dealer. For her to involve the police and retain her integrity, nothing less than an original McCubbin could be used. And since our only intention was to uncover who murdered Pamela, rather than any associated art fraud, can't we, as businessmen come to some arrangement to ensure that the police believe that Mullet was responsible for Pamela's murder?'

Karen sighed at the audacity of Clay's suggestion. Clay flashed her a knowing look to keep her quiet.

'What sort of arrangement do you have in mind?' Scarlet asked, displaying abject disinterest.

'Well, if you were to let us go, we would promise not to involve you. We could tell the police that Karen and I killed Mullet in our efforts to escape. We could argue that Mullet abducted Karen to eliminate her because Karen came looking for her friend Pam, whom he had already killed and that I broke into this garage to rescue Karen, after following Mullet here. After all, as you said, Mullet did all this off his own bat.'

Karen groaned. Clay looked over and saw that Karen's shaking and shallow gasping had abated. Maybe Karen has become somewhat conditioned against shock by repeated exposure to disaster. Karen was looking at Clay with one eye and gently shaking her head in amazement at Clay's latest proposal.

Scarlet started to laugh; he laughed so hard he almost choked. When he stopped laughing, he said, 'I have no leverage in a deal like that. There is nothing to stop you from giving me up the minute I let you go.'

'What about the painting?' Clay asked, growing ever more desperate to find an angle. 'We could give you the painting, which would more than cover any loss if you had to withdraw from Australia —'

'— Give it a rest Clay,' Karen said, a bleak tone pervading her interjection, 'He's not interested in a deal that is going to leave any evidence that might lead the police to him. Mullet's body is a dead giveaway because Mullet worked at B.S Fine Art.'

'I'm afraid the little lady is correct,' Scarlet said.

While Clay was bargaining, Scarlet had removed two lengths of seatbelt webbing, like those used by Mullet to suspend the fatal engine blocks, from a nearby bin. He then ordered Karen to strap Clay's arms to his sides and finished by strapping Clay and Karen together, sitting back-to-back.

Clay fell silent as their options evaporated. When Scarlet left to search the flame store after piling empty cardboard cartons, oily rags and old tyres around Mullet, Clay asked Karen if she was okay. Karen didn't answer, so he asked her what she thought Scarlet was up to.

'I think he intends to torch the place with us inside,' Karen replied, her voice laden with hopelessness. 'Three burnt, unidentifiable bodies, will leave little useful evidence for the police to connect any of this mess to him. Clay watched solemnly as Scarlet emerged from the flame store with a small drum of lacquer thinners.

Still searching for a way out, and at the very least playing for time Clay said, 'What will you gain with further murders?'

Scarlet paused. 'You're a persistent bugger, Weston; I'll give you that. I'm not going to explain my motives, all I'll say, is that you and your girlfriend unwittingly stumbled into my money laundering operation, which is much bigger than you could ever imagine.'

Clay again marvelled at the criminal's need to exhibit the fruits of his labour. As an artist Clay was able to, in fact was expected to, exhibit. The crook, however, suffered an unrequited need to bask in the glow of his own perceived brilliance.

'You see, Clay, I use the opaque nature of the art market when it comes to purchases and valuations, to disguise the transfer of dirty money into art assets. Assets that can be moved around the world with very few questions being asked.'

'What about the fake Streeton's I saw? How do they fit in?'

'All part of the cover. You don't think I'm going to waste money on genuine paintings, do you?'

Clay nodded, he was running out of time-wasting questions and gave Karen an imploring look. Karen turned away from Clay refusing to engage.

Clay returned his attention to Scarlet.

'Listen, Barry,' Clay said, desperately trying to attract the attention of Scarlet, who was busy scouring the workshop for flammable items. 'How about you employ me to paint some fakes for you? I'd be unlikely to involve the police if I was also involved in the fraud.'

'Wow, you are getting desperate Clay,' Scarlet, said with a grin as he piled armfuls of old newspapers on and around some old tyres he'd previously piled around Mullet's body. 'It's all a bit, what if, don't you think? I'd be wondering all the time, whether you'd managed to come up with some angle that would enable you to safely go to the police.'

Clay could see that his constant arguments and creative suggestions were becoming more and more implausible, even dangerous. The two men stared silently at each other, Scarlet with a look of regret at the loss of a possible gain, and Clay with an element of resignation, despite his effort to mask it.

Chapter Twenty-Five

A knock at the side entrance door interrupted Scarlet's preparations. Scarlet swung around and stared at the door. Clay and Karen held their breath. Scarlet pulled his pistol from his pocket, turned toward his captives, held a silencing finger up to his lips and pushed his pistol into Karen's face.

'One word and your girlfriend is dead,' Scarlet whispered to Clay.

'Hello. Is anyone there? Are you there, Clay?' Julia's voice issued from behind the side entrance door.

Clay's surprise was mingled with both relief and apprehension. He was relieved that Scarlet had been interrupted and that the game had changed, but worried by the danger Julia was about to walk into.

Clay watched the door swing open. Julia stepped through and paused just inside the entrance, waiting for her eyes to adjust to the gloom. It was now late afternoon, so less light was available to illuminate the interior of the workshop from the overhead skylights.

'I thought I heard voices. Is that you, Clay?' Julia asked, advancing slowly into the workshop still waiting for her eyes to fully adjust.

Julia froze.

'My God!' she said, suddenly seeing Mullet's bloody body. Clay and Karen sat silently on the workshop floor, partially obscured behind the pile of engine blocks that had maimed Mullet. Scarlet had retreated into the shadows as Julia entered. He now stepped forward into view, his pistol prominent.

'That's Terry, my assistant,' Scarlet said. 'I'm afraid he met with a rather unfortunate accident. I presume you are Julia Blakely, the director of the Blakely Gallery. I'm Barry Scarlet of B.S. Fine Art, but I'm sure you don't require an introduction.' Scarlet gave a little bow. 'Nice of you to drop by to view my new McCubbin,' Scarlet said, with the sweep of his free hand. 'Now be a good girl and sit down on the floor next to your pals.'

Julia advanced further into the workshop at the point of Scarlet's pistol.

Clay looked up at Julia with an ashen smile.

'Hi Julia, join the disaster,' Karen said, shaking her messy hair from her eyes.

Julia did not react to the bruised and dishevelled appearance of her friends; instead, she scuffed at the dirty concrete floor with her fashionable heels and addressed Scarlet.

'Do I have to sit on this filthy floor?'

Clay was surprised at Julia's brashness, in view of their predicament. Clay wondered what she was up to.

'Be my guest,' Scarlet said, waving his pistol in the direction of the chair Clay had been chained to earlier. 'When you are comfortable, perhaps you could tell me how you managed to find this place.'

'Clay phoned me this morning and told me he'd followed your late assistant to a vacant auto shop in the street behind his studio in Cotton Lane. Clay told me he suspected that Karen might be imprisoned there. I didn't have to be Mrs. Sherlock Holmes to find the place; all I needed was a Melways.'

'Seems the whole world knows about Terry's secret fucking bolt hole,' Scarlet said, beginning an agitated shuffle.

'Yes. Everyone knows, including the police. They also know that you are wanted for questioning by Interpol in Europe.'

Scarlet stopped pacing, and Clay could see by his twitchy expression and the white-knuckled grip on his pistol that Julia's confident exposition was biting.

'Is that so?' Scarlet suddenly lurched forward and slapped Julia hard across the face. Julia just managed to remain seated on the chair, but when she turned back to face Scarlet, Clay could see that some of her confidence had evaporated. Julia's voice now trembled, and she shied away as if expecting a second assault when she added her final barb.

'Your precious McCubbin is worthless!'

'I don't believe you!' Scarlet screamed. 'Why? How?

'Clay painted it.'

'I don't believe you.' He retrieved the painting for a second examination. After a minute, he gave Clay a fierce interrogative stare.

With a weak smile, Clay nodded in the affirmative.

Scarlet stamped his foot, threw his head back and glared up at the skylight, the veins in his neck pulsing with anger. By the skylight's waning light, illumination began to dawn.

'If this picture isn't genuine, then all along, you were using it to bait me.' He paused, allowing his words to clot. 'Hence the involvement of the police. More than likely the Fraud Squad.' Anger and frustration rippled through Scarlet's body. 'And I thought you lot were only trying to discover who killed your model friend.'

Scarlet glowered, alternating his gaze between the painting and his captives. When he spoke again, his voice exuded an icy determination. Clay felt a trickle of cold sweat run down his flanks as he realised that the time for negotiating was over.

'If the police really are aware of this place, then I have no options. I need to eliminate all evidence of Terry's stuff up,' Scarlet said, with callous indifference.

Placing the McCubbin painting to one side, Scarlet swung into action. He threatened Julia with his pistol and the raised back of his hand to remain seated, which she did, her earlier audacity now curtailed by Scarlet's blatant violence. Scarlet then completed his preparations for arson by pouring some of the paint thinners he'd retrieved from the flame store over the pile of flammable material he'd gathered and piled around Mullet's body. Scarlet completed his preparations by stuffing an oily rag in the neck of the can of thinners to act as a wick.

Clay sat quietly searching his brain for something to say to deflect or delay Scarlet. Karen sat with her head down staring at the floor and Julia sat silently following Scarlet's preparations occasionally checking her delicate gold wristwatch.

'Time's up my friends,' Scarlet said, as he retrieved the McCubbin. 'Looks like I can't risk returning to B.S. Fine Art and bumping into the Fraud Squad, so fake or not, this little picture should finance my departure. Meanwhile, this fire should provide a suitable diversion.'

Clay said nothing. Karen sighed. And Julia checked her watch again.

Scarlet laughed,

'What! Nothing to say, Mr. Weston?'

Then Scarlet pulled an oxy-torch flint lighter from his jacket pocket, which he'd found on a shelf at the back of the workshop. He gathered the detritus for his bonfire and bent down to spark the lighter on the rag wick. Nothing happened. Most of the thinners had evaporated. Scarlet tried again on the flap of one of the cardboard boxes he'd doused, but still no luck.

'Fuck!' Scarlet cursed, flinging the spark lighter across the workshop.

Clay smiled. As a painter, he knew how volatile lacquer thinners were. Scarlet's error was to spread the contents of the drum, allowing it to quickly evaporate.

Julia checked her watch again.

Scarlet stood back and scanned the workshop, which was now quite dark, for an alternative ignition source. He looked down at Mullet and started kicking at his body in a sudden burst of exasperated rage. Mid kick he stopped and bent down with a smirk on his face and rifled through Mullet's jacket. Out came a pack of cigarettes followed by Mullet's lighter.

Clay groaned.

Julia checked her watch again. The vacant automotive shop had become a crepuscular space.

Scarlet smiled and bent down to use the cigarette lighter.

Chapter Twenty-Six

The side access door burst open. Senior Constable Parker slipped through the opening and slid sideways to allow a second officer to join her. Their torches probed the dull garage workshop interior. The kaleidoscope of ghostly light circles reminded Clay of a St. Kilda Luna Park ghost train ride.

Scarlet flicked his lit cigarette lighter into the pile of cardboard boxes, snatched up Clay's fake McCubbin and sprinted across the workshop into the oily shadows behind a palette of old tyres.

Clay anxiously watched the lighter flame flicker amongst the boxes.

'Scarlet's got a gun!' Julia's yell punctuated the darkness.

Constable Parker and the officer dropped into a crouch. Their torch beams converged towards the sound of Julia's warning, lighting the three captives long enough to understand their situation.

'Stay down,' Parker ordered, taking note of the fire taking hold in the pile of debris nearby. 'Barry Scarlet, this is the police. Drop your weapon and step forward with your hands above your head.'

The crack of Scarlet's pistol answered Parker's request.

Clay, Karen and Julia cringed more closely together on the cold concrete floor. Parker and her offsider snapped off their torches and ducked sideways. Scarlet's bullet showered Parker with brick fragments from the wall behind.

Both officers drew their service revolvers. At the same time, Scarlet's diversionary bonfire flamed up with a shower of sparks. The workshop was filled with eerie flickering shadows. Scarlet's shadowed form danced into indistinct relief, to reveal him working his way along the side wall towards the entrance.

'Drop your weapon or we will fire!' Parker yelled from behind a solid timber crate filled with old gearboxes.

Scarlet, his position revealed, quickened his pace towards the side entrance. As he moved, he sprayed a volley of shots in the direction of the officers.

Parker's offsider fired twice. One bullet slammed into Scarlet's right shoulder spinning him around. He grunted in pain and retreated. He now brandished his pistol in his left hand. Parker stepped from behind her cover, and with perfect shooting range composure, placed a bullet into Scarlet's left thigh. Scarlet screamed, jerked to the left and slumped to one knee. He managed to hold onto his pistol, which he attempted to aim at Parker.

'Drop your weapon!' Parker ordered.

Although contorted with pain, a scowl formed on Scarlet's face, as he struggled for a bead on Parker.

A final shot from the other officer clipped the elbow of Scarlet's wavering left arm, jerking the pistol free from his murderous grip. Scarlet slumped to the concrete, swearing.

The fire, although contained to the bundled rubbish was beginning to fill the workshop with smoke.

Parker crouched low and waded into the smoke. She met the three captives crawling towards the exit.

'What kept you?' Julia asked, when she saw Senior Constable Parker emerge from the smoke.

'What?' Clay's mouth dropped open on hearing Julia's question. Julia ignored Clay's surprise.

'Detective Walsh was reluctant to allocate resources,' Parker answered coolly.

After Scarlet vanished into the shadows to effect his escape, Julia untied Clay, and then they both released Karen. They all dropped to the concrete when the gunfight began.

Behind them, the fire exploded with a burst of light that silhouetted the three of them. Enveloped in billowing black smoke, Scarlet cursed and screamed blame at Mullet's corpse, as if bludgeoning him to death had not been enough.

As soon as they had all tumbled out of the building into the fresh air, Parker ordered her constable to call in the fire brigade. Behind them, a narrow column of flame shattered a skylight, showering the workshop floor with glass and spraying Melbourne's dusky ultramarine sky with sparks.

'Seems your intuition regarding Weston panned out Parker,'

Parker turned at the sound of Detective Walsh's voice, ignored the detective's patronising comment and said,

'Scarlet's still inside wounded. If we don't get the prick out, he'll be toast and we'll lose any chance of wrapping up this stuff up.'

Detective Walsh paled at Parker's implied criticism, but he stepped forward and opened the door for her. The fire roared, appreciating the inrush of oxygen. Then, they both took a deep breath and dived back into the workshop.

'Watch yourself, Boss, Scarlet's armed,' Clay heard Parker say, as they ducked beneath the acrid smoke billowing from the open doorway.

Scarlet's paint-blistering cursing had ceased, and after what seemed like an inordinate wait, the door burst back open, and Parker and Walsh dragged a semi-conscious, bloodied Scarlet from the burning building.

'Will he live?' Clay asked, concerned that Scarlet's demise might make his case for innocence difficult to prosecute.

'I hope he fucking dies,' Karen answered, shaking with a combination of cold, shock and anger. She looked like she could kick him to death, if free to do so.

'Don't think so.' Parker said, between gasps for clear air. 'I reckon he's unconscious due to a combination of pain, blood loss and smoke.'

Two fire engines, their sirens jangling, slid into the curb in front of the burning auto shop, joined almost immediately by an ambulance, and Dover Street was suddenly filled with activity.

Dazed and slumped on the footpath on the other side of Dover Street, Clay, Karen and Julia watched in silence as the emergency services extinguished the fire, treated Scarlet, bundled him into an ambulance with a couple of police officers and started to tape off the crime scene. Their stupor was broken only by the approach of Senior Constable Parker.

'You guys are free to go. We'll be in touch to get your statements when we've questioned Scarlet.' Then wagging a finger at Clay, she added with a grin, 'Don't you go leaving Melbourne.'

'What? Who? Me?' Clay stuttered, his hands stretched out palm up, gesturing innocence.

'Shut up, Clay,' Karen said, rolling her eyes at Julia before swiftly changing the subject. 'God, I stink. I need a shower.'

'You could use my bathroom,' Clay said, trying to regain a little approbation. 'My studio is just around the corner in Cotton Lane.'

'I think Karen needs a little more pampering than your garret shower, Clay.' Clay looked at Julia confused.

Julia waived his suggestion away with a pointed query. 'Is your bathroom still littered with tins of dirty paintbrushes hoping to share your soap?'

Clay answered with a sick expression. He looked hard at Julia. Was she implying that he was making a play for Karen's attention or was she mad at him for the Scarlet-Mullet disaster? Clay wasn't sure because Julia turned away to offer Karen her newly renovated bathroom with an expansive claw foot bath and spare bedroom at Type Street.

'Thank you, Julia, yes please.' The two women rose to their feet leaving Clay hunched on the footpath. 'I can't wait to get out of these clothes and wash the stink of that man off me.'

'Clay?'

'No,' Karen said, looking down at Clay as if in doubt. 'That other disgusting creature, Mullet.'

Both girls laughed as if some private joke had suddenly become public.

'Come on then, my BMW is parked down the road. Do you need a lift to your studio, Clay?' Julia asked curtly as she turned to walk to her car.

'I guess not. After all, my place is just around the corner.' Feeling deflated, Clay climbed to his feet and ruefully watched the two girls disappear down Dover Street towards Julia's car, arm in arm.

Chapter Twenty-Seven

Slightly perplexed, Clay watched the two women depart south down Dover Street in Julia's BMW, their departure accompanied by a feeling of isolation and rejection. Clay sagged back against the cement factory wall behind him, using it for support. No thanks from the police for fingering Scarlet and tracking down Mullet. No gratitude from Karen for taking three hits to the head and neck, numerous kicks and punches from Mullet and ultimately saving her skin.

Clay was still pondering his situation and forlornly gazing south down an empty Dover Street when his mood was interrupted. A fireman wanting to execute a three-point turn, shouted from the fire engine's cab for him to move out of the way. Clay jumped at the unexpected request, the sudden exertion triggering a bevy of aches and pain in his head and neck as well as unexpected twinges in other strained muscles. Clay groaned, the jabs of pain snapping him back to reality. He now noticed that all the police had left the scene and that a second man from the last remaining fire truck was trying to close the front sliding door to the partially destroyed auto workshop.

'Hold on for a second mate,' Clay said, walking towards the fireman while massaging the back of his neck. 'My backpack with my wallet and house keys is still inside. I wonder if I could retrieve it before you close up.'

The fireman hauling on the sliding door stopped and looked at Clay, no doubt trying to assess the validity of Clay's request. Clay could see by the fireman's expression that his battered appearance elicited some sympathy.

'Please,' was all Clay needed to add for the fireman to nod, pull back the door and wave him through.

'You'll need this,' was all he said, handing Clay a large battery torch.

Inside the workshop, his torch illuminated evidence markers and pools of water that filled depressions in the uneven concrete floor including the pit under the hoist. The sound of water dripping into these pools from the charred rafters, the acrid smell of burnt rubber and oil and the silent evidence markers standing like gravestones, contrasted the terror the garage had encompassed during their ordeal.

With the aid of the torch, Clay picked his way across the garage floor towards the flame store, skirting the pile of engine blocks that had pinned the unfortunate Mullet.

Near the flame store door Clay easily found his empty backpack, but what he really wanted to retrieve, was the fake McCubbin. Clay knew it had to be near where Scarlet had made his final stand with the police.

Evidence markers left by the police now marked the position on the garage floor where Scarlet had lain. With a quick search near the markers, Clay discovered his painting leaning against the wall that led to the side entrance, behind a stack of pallets. Clay stuffed the painting into his backpack, and seeing that his wallet was still inside, he pulled it out before heading back towards the fireman.

'Thanks mate,' Clay said, handing back the torch and waving his wallet aloft. 'My studio keys are inside this wallet, so you've saved me a heap of grief.'

'Happy to help, just don't mention to Walsh that I let you tamper with the site evidence.' The fireman tapped the side of his nose, and Clay nodded to acknowledge he understood, before heading north towards Richmond Station.

Clay's intention was to walk around the block into Cubitt Street and on to his studio in Cotton Lane. It was now just before 10 PM and the sounds of Melbourne's quieter night ambience mingled with a balmy spring temperature a few degrees above the average, made for a pleasant walk.

By the time Clay reached Cubitt Street, the walk had loosened Clay's sore and stiffened muscles. A rumbling stomach reminded Clay that he hadn't eaten since his early morning breakfast at Red's pub in Brighton. He changed his mind about returning directly to his studio and turned to head for 'The Chicken Bar' in Swan Street. With every step Clay not only felt physically better, but knowing he was off the hook for Pamela's murder gave him an added psychological boost. Clay walked with the consoling thought that his life would now return to normal.

On the way to 'The Chicken Bar' Clay decided to give Julia a quick ring. Clay felt their relationship had become tense and if his work and life were to return to normal, he wanted to smooth things out with her. He also wanted to find out how and why Julia had turned up at the garage with the police not far behind. Clay figured Julia should be home by now, so a call from one of the public telephones at Richmond Station should do the trick.

Julia's home phone rang on for so long that Clay feared she had gone out or to bed.

'Hello, Julia Blakely here, who is calling please?'

'It's Clay, Julia. I'm glad I caught you.'

'Oh, it's you. What do you want Clay? It's getting late,' Julia said, with a distinctly antipathetic tone.

'I just want to arrange a meeting with you at the gallery tomorrow.'

After a longer than expected pause, Julia replied.

'I suppose tomorrow's okay. I don't have my diary with me, but you can wait if I have another client in my office. I'll expect you at 10.30'.

'All right, I'll see you then,' Clay said, but Julia had hung up. Clay stared at the handpiece in disbelief, before replacing it on the hook.

The takeaway chicken box warmed Clay's hands, but his studio when he entered felt cold and discomforting. Stalled at the entrance, Clay scanned his home space trying to decide where to sit and eat. His usual battered but comfortable lounge chair still occupied its same position in front of his primary easel. But it was now loaded with sketchbooks, scraps of canvas and paint rags, all the result of his hurried clean-up prior to leaving for Sydney when Pamela first went missing. Memories of lounging in his favourite armchair, lost in contemplation of his latest work seemed distant. An uneasy shiver coursed through Clay. His beloved studio space felt alien.

Clay paced around his studio, eating chicken from the takeaway box. He pulled out and examined the paintings from his current series, the series he was soon to exhibit at Julia's Blakely Gallery. The paintings were mostly figure pieces using Pamela as the model. Painted over the course of the last year, they examined his painterly interpretation of W. B Yeats's poem of Leda and the Swan. Yeats suggested in his poem that the mythology 'Leda and the Swan' demonstrated the constantly changing nature of experience as opposed to the frozen aesthetic provided by a painting. When Clay stood back and examined this group of paintings now spread around his studio, he felt uneasy. It wasn't simply his studio space that now felt alien, but that same feeling now extended to these paintings. They looked remote, academic and incongruous.

Clay tossed aside the takeaway chicken carton, emptied the contents of his easy chair to the floor and slumped into it, somewhat disconcerted and bewildered by these new feelings. Clay's backpack fell to the floor as he cleared the chair, and he noticed the fake McCubbin spill from it.

Reaching down, Clay picked up the painting and examined it. Instantly, pleasurable memories of his time spent creating the picture at Brighton Beach flooded through him. Why did this fake elicit such satisfaction and contentment? The painting was not only irrelevant to his current work, but the entire contemporary art scene, and yet the act of painting it had provided the most satisfying experience he'd had in ages. Clay decided that his current low mood was a natural response to his tired and battered body. The entire crazy experience of the past few weeks had resulted in an underlying state of shock.

A hot shower and a good night's sleep are what I need, Clay thought. Also, Julia will sort things out in the morning when I see her.

Chapter Twenty-Eight

Clay chose to walk to Blakely Gallery for his meeting with Julia. He needed time to think. A night of fitful dream-riddled sleep had only partly revived his mood. Yesterday's concerns about his painting practice still lingered. Clay was starting to wonder if his recent near-death experience had precipitated a career crisis. Why did he still feel out of place in his studio? Clay wondered; as he returned the paintings, he'd pulled from his storage racks the previous night, and why did these paintings still oddly look like someone else's work?

When Clay picked up the fake McCubbin to stow it, the painting's refreshing effect on him was still evident. On the spur of the moment, Clay packed the painting into his backpack to take with him. He wanted Julia's opinion of the picture. Maybe she could help him understand his response to the painting.

Clay left for Blakely Gallery with a niggling level of anxiety, but also with the hope that the swirl of disconcerting questions in his mind would soon be resolved.

As Clay walked, he reflected on his haphazard entry into the world of high art. He'd never deliberately or intentionally chosen an art career. An act of defiance or an adolescent desire for independence may have been his initial motivation, but these reasons now seemed poor justifications for the choices he'd made. He could have chosen to surf, enjoyed the distraction the waves offered, and become a 'surfing bum' as Harold would say. Clay had to admit that art school and painting exhibitions had provided an acceptable option. He also had to admit that he hadn't strained in his endeavours. His success had come very easily.

The heavy wooden door to Blakely Gallery looked strangely daunting as Clay approached. Clay hoped that the hollow feeling in the pit of his stomach was the result of not having bothered with breakfast, rather than anxiety over an existential crisis with his art. Clay paused at the door and took a deep breath before pushing on into the gallery.

In the foyer, Clay looked across toward Julia's glass-walled office. He immediately saw both Julia and Karen, their heads together, deep in excited discussion and occasionally laughing. Neither woman noticed Clay until he was standing at the entrance to Julia's office.

'Oh, Hi Clay,' Julia said, looking up and motioning Clay towards an empty chair beside Karen. Karen stopped giggling, looked around at Clay, and nodded.

'How are you, Clay?' Julia asked.

'Physically, not bad,' Clay said, choosing not to mention his underlying mental unease. 'A few bruises and some muscles are a bit stiff,' Clay said, removing his backpack before lowering himself into the chair beside Karen.

'I said I was sorry about clocking you. What was it? Three times?' Karen said, turning to face Clay with a cheeky grin.

'Let's hope you knocked some sense into him,' Julia said, with a conspiratorial chuckle.

'It's a good thing I have a hard head,' Clay said, rubbing the back of his head. Out of the corner of his eye, Clay caught the merest of smiles on Julia's lips.

'Are you sure it's not simply a thick skull?' Karen said, with a wink at Julia.

Clay stared at Karen, unsure how to respond. Was she serious or joking?

'Well, you did take a while to acknowledge the seriousness of Pam's situation,' Karen added, responding to his incredulous look. Karen followed up with another glance at Julia as if they were in agreement.

Clay fell silent, gazed up into the gallery rafters and took a few deep breaths. He wondered what sort of tete-a-tete he'd interrupted when he arrived.

'You called me last night to arrange this meeting, Clay. What issue is it you want to discuss?' Julia asked.

'I don't know. They're not really issues. I thought... I thought we could have a friendly get-together, debrief, and commiserate. Whatever?'

Julia straightened in her chair and gave Clay a slightly jaded look as if he might be wasting her time.

'Well, to start with,' Clay said, 'I wondered how you turned up at the old auto shop in Dover Street in the nick of time?'

'Simple, Clay. When you rang that morning and told me about the state of Karen's flat, your subsequent run-in with Mullet and Scarlet at B.S. Fine Art, and what you'd learnt from Harold about Scarlet's criminal background, I became worried.

Worried that your amateur sleuthing was getting way out of hand. So, when you failed to turn up later that morning with the fake McCubbin, I decided to ring the police. I spoke with S.C. Jenny Parker. She told me, that her enquiries indicated Scarlett might have some-how been involved with Pamela's disappearance. I told Parker, that you believed Karen was being held in a dis-used auto garage, located somewhere near your studio. Parker thought she knew the auto shop you mentioned because she regularly patrolled that part of Richmond. Parker indicated to me, that she needed a couple of hours to organise the logistics of a search and get approval from her senior officer, Detective Walsh, to investigate. When Parker rang back and told me she'd organised a raid for early that evening, I waited initially, then decided, against Parker's advice "to leave it to the police," in favour of looking for myself. The rest you know.'

Julia gave Clay a there-you-have-it look.

'But! I did do the wrong thing, Clay. I behaved like you. I turned up at that garage and nearly got myself killed.'

'I must say though, Julia,' Karen said, nodding toward Clay for agreement. 'I'm very glad you turned up when you did because you were able to untie us when the police arrived.

Clay smiled at Karen, thankful for her engagement and small measure of support.

Julia acknowledged Karen's gratitude with a nod but quickly turned back to address Clay.

'Mention of police involvement brings me to my main concern regarding this affair.'

'Yeah, I agree with you Julia. It was foolish of me to try to save Karen and clear myself. I guess I'm just that sort of impulsive guy.' Clay gave Karen a quick smirk before continuing. 'But Julia. Karen is alive. I'm off the hook, totally innocent, and had nothing to do with Pamela's demise. —'

'—No, No, Clay. You don't get it. My main concern is that stupid fake McCubbin you cooked up.' Julia rolled her eyes before continuing. 'If the police find that painting and start asking questions, then my gallery's reputation will be trashed.'

Clay laughed.

Julia stared daggers at him.

'Keep your hair on, Julia, your gallery's safe. I have the painting here.' Clay gave his backpack a quick pat. 'I retrieved it from the garage last night before I returned to my studio.'

'Now now children,' Karen chimed in, trying to diffuse the situation. Clay beamed at Karen thinking she was on his side with the rescue bid.

'I probably would have been okay Clay, if you hadn't poked your head into my line of fire,' Karen said, with a serious look. 'Because Julia did have the cops lined up.'

The two women smiled at each other indicating complete agreement.

Clay felt isolated and sick. At the same time, he realised that Julia was not interested in seeing his McCubbin, only in making sure it was buried. Julia turned back to Clay.

'On a related matter, I think it would be a good idea to push your upcoming October exhibition date on twelve to eighteen months. That would allow time for all the publicity about this incident to die down. Art fraud and murder don't sit well with my clients.'

Clay's jaw dropped.

'But, but... I had nothing to do with Pamela's death, I'm totally innocent...' Clay said, his voice trailing to silence.

'It's got nothing to do with guilt or innocence, Clay, it's simply a matter of painting the right publicity image.'

All the doubts Clay felt about his current work swirled through his mind as the commercial reality underpinning his artistic career hit home. Clay didn't hear much of Julia's revised exhibition timetable or her suggestions on how to take a low public profile. For a few seconds that seemed like minutes, Clay unsuccessfully tried to make sense of his own mounting anxieties.

'Clay! Are you listening?' Julia said, slapping the top of her desk to gain his attention.

'Uhh! What? Yes, I am,' Clay said, trying to marshal his thoughts. But after a few seconds of floundering for an appropriate response, Clay asked, 'What did you just say, Julia?'

'I said, I've asked Karen to become my assistant at the gallery.'

'Oh! Really.'

'Yes, and one of her jobs will be to manage publicity and liaise with my stable of artists.

'But what am I supposed to do during this low-profile period?' Clay asked, gripping the arms of his chair and gazing straight at Julia, his tangled thoughts becoming vocal.

'Well, that's up to you Clay, you're the artist. I only sell the stuff you come up with.'

Clay squirmed in his seat at Julia's description of his artwork as stuff. He looked across the desk trying to read Julia's expression, and saw her, for the first time without the personal veil of desire he'd always viewed her through. An attitude he now realised he'd maintained since their art school intimacy. Clay now saw the fierce pecuniary expression of a focused business-woman.

'I've drafted a contract, outlining our mutual responsibilities for your exhibition and management,' Julia said, pushing a folder of documents across her desk toward Clay.

'What happened to our handshake agreement,' Clay said, his voice cracking.

'I've been meaning to tidy up our relationship for quite a while. It's been a bit messy because you were my first artist client when I opened the gallery. Now that we manage a stable of twelve artists, things are different.'

Disappointment surged through Clay. He felt embarrassed and foolish.

'Things sure are different,' Clay said. 'I'm no longer a friend. Now I'm a client that needs managing?' Clay's earlier apprehension, uncertainty and anxiety regarding his life and career spiked.

'I suppose... I could try to finish my current series of paintings,' Clay stammered. 'Even start over with a new series. But now, I don't even have a model. I'd need a replacement.'

Clay turned towards Karen.

Karen who'd been sitting quietly nodding in agreement with Julia while examining her nail polish, quickly responded to Clay's implied offer.

'No, no. Don't look at me!' Karen said, holding her hands up as if symbolically pushing Clay away. 'Now that I'm working with Julia, I can't appear to favour any one artist in our stable over any other. Also, I don't think it would be appropriate for me to appear naked in a painting when I'm discussing purchases with gallery customers.'

It seemed to Clay that the events of recent days had coalesced to deliver the equivalent of an early mid-life crisis - a fork in the road. Clay gave Karen a fragile smile.

Clay stood up and slid the contract folder back across Julia's desk.

'I think I'll pass on this,' Clay said, noticing a distinct lack of surprise on Julia's face.

Clay grabbed his backpack and headed for the door with the growing feeling he was finally taking the right path.

'Maybe I'll see you around, Julia,' Clay said over his shoulder.

Both women soundlessly watched Clay leave.

Acknowledgments

I would like to thank my wife, Julie for reading early drafts, providing pertinent advice and generally putting up with my artistic pique. Without her love and support, I would never have made it to the finish line.

As a long-time member of the Goulburn Valley Writer's Group, I also would like to thank the members of this group for encouraging me to continue, listening to and providing valuable feedback over the lengthy gestation period for sections of my manuscript.

A very special thanks to my first reader and editor, Helena Kilfoyle for her valuable time, energy and encouragement given to me to make this publication a reality. Without her suggestions, corrections and boundless knowledge of language and usage I would have been unable to complete this novel to the standard required.

About the Author

Creagh has previously published short stories and poetry in literary journals. As an avid reader of crime fiction, Creagh has broadened his writing practice with this debut crime novel. Creagh is an artist and teacher who currently resides in central Victoria Australia. He spends his time painting, writing and tending his garden.